M000202469

Walk with Me Through Alaska

Charley Dunn

PublishAmerica
Baltimore

First printing

ISBN: 1-4241-9028-2
PUBLISHED BY PUBLISHAMERICA, LLLP
www.publishamerica.com
Baltimore

Printed in the United States of America

About the Author

My name is Charley Dunn I was born in Henderson, Texas, on October 7, 1940. My wife and I met and married in Norman, Oklahoma. We were married on November 29, 1960. My wife's maiden name is Janet Isaacs. We have two daughters and one son. Both of our daughters were born in Norman, Oklahoma. Our son was born in Soldotna, Alaska. My family moved to Alaska in 1966, and we are still living here today, except for our youngest daughter who now lives in Florida.

I would like to dedicate this book to my wife Janet. She has shown an extraordinary amount of patience, without which I would not have been able to do the things depicted in this book. She worked and kept our home along with raising our three children practically alone. I still wonder how she was able to put up with my being gone so much, sometimes for prolonged periods of time. It takes a special kind of woman to do what she has done, and my love for her grows stronger with each passing day.

Acknowledgments

I would like to acknowledge a loving God, for protecting me and giving me the wisdom to know what to do when things happened that could have ended very differently than they did. It's a wonder to me that I have survived at all and still have all of my fingers and toes. So for all of this and things to come, I give thanks to him daily.

My family has supported my work on this book, and I would like to thank them for their support, especially my son and daughter in-law, Tessa, who proof read and made suggestions that helped me to complete it. To my wife, who once again has shown great patience while I spent hours at my computer writing. I would also like to thank all of my friends who have given me permission to use their names and the names of their family members in my book.

This poem was written for me and presented to me by one of the operators who worked for me. I would like to share it with you.

Transition

When restlessness in heart and soul,
Stirs to life a hidden role,
A yearn to do what others dream,
A foolish quest at first it seems,

Some may laugh and criticize,
Before they ever realize,
That little is handed out for free,
They dwell in false security,

But when the goal is set afire,
The determination will inspire,
To plot a course and see it through,
And not look back until you do,

To give up all that you may own,
To leave behind your kin and home,
Is no small sacrifice, you see,
For doubts en route to tranquility,

Follow your rainbows, stars, or dreams,
It's great to be at freedom's streams,
Without attempting you may never know,
Where the green, green grasses, really grow.

Vision the future, recall last spring,
What you seek is something to cling,
You can reach fulfillment in all of your plans,
Just look to the heavens; it's all in his hands.

By Dave Thompson

Foreword
Going to Alaska

It's amazing how a simple phone call can change your life sometimes forever.

My family and I were living in Denver, Colorado, and we had never thought about living anywhere else.

My wife's family was living in Soldotna, Alaska. Her dad had called to tell us about a job opportunity with a local drilling company. We decided that this was a good chance to get ahead since the wages offered by this company were much better than what I was getting in Denver.

My wife and I decided that I would go first and get established so she and our two little girls would have a place to live when they got here. Our plan was to stay for two years and then return to Denver. After the two years had passed we found that we couldn't leave Alaska, so we stayed and made a life for our family here.

If I had it to do over again I wouldn't change a thing. Moving to Alaska turned out to be the best thing I have ever done. I didn't realize it at the time, but I was going to have more adventure than I could possibly have imagined.

I came to Alaska on my birthday, October 7, 1965. I was twenty-five, and my wife was twenty-four. And so this is how my lifetime of adventure in Alaska started.

Flying to Alaska in 1965 was quite an experience. It was the first time I had ever flown any distance, and it seemed like I would never get there. I boarded an airplane at Stapleton International airport in Denver. The first stop was Seattle, Washington, where I was transferred to an Alaska-bound plane. The trip to Anchorage from Seattle was long and uneventful, and we arrived on schedule.

This is when I began to think I might have made a mistake. At the Anchorage terminal we were led out to the plane through a tunnel made of plywood. The plane we boarded was a prop-driven super Connie, the type used by the military for troop transport in the early sixties. Apparently our luggage was already on the plane, and it took off heading to Kenai, Alaska.

The trip was okay, but you couldn't see much because it was dark. It must have been around eight or nine in the evening when the plane began its decent into Kenai. I couldn't see a terminal, and the runway lights didn't look right. I could see car lights but not much more. When the plane landed and we had deplaned I started looking for the terminal. I couldn't find it, so I asked someone where it was. His comment to me was, "Over there, buddy."

What I saw really shook me. It was a small building, about twelve feet wide by twelve feet long, made out of plywood. I asked one of the people inside where I could find my luggage his comment only added to my confusion. He said, "Where it always is. It's out there."

When I looked in the direction he had indicated I saw that the luggage was piled on the ground under the plane, and it was snowing. About this time my mother and father-in-law met up with me, and I told them that if I had the money, I would get on that plane and go back to Denver. I had five dollars in my pocket at the time, or I would have done just that.

The trip from the Kenai airport to Soldotna was eleven miles, and as we drove along I noticed there weren't any street lights; for that matter there weren't many lights at all. The narrow road was covered with snow, and it was bumpy. When we arrived in Soldotna it was the same; there weren't many lights, and the roads were still bumpy.

At my in-law's home we unloaded my baggage then went into the front of a church and down to the basement where they lived. My father-in-law was the pastor of the Soldotna Church of God located at the corner of Redout Street and Binkley Avenue. They came to Alaska in 1964 just after the Good Friday earthquake. The next morning I found out that the job I had came to Alaska to get had been filled by someone else. Apparently I had arrived a day later than I was supposed to.

My wife and children joined me in Alaska in the spring of 1966, and we settled in the township of Soldotna, Alaska. Soldotna and Kenai were very small communities in 1966; there were no malls, fast food restaurants, or large grocery stores. There were a few service stations, all without convenience stores. The Soldotna post office had about seven hundred boxes for rent. Ours was box 596. There were no stop lights anywhere on the Kenai Peninsula at this time. Most of the roads were not paved and were sometimes muddy and rough. Some of the main highways were paved, but they were narrow and curvy. Soldotna became a first-class city in 1967 and has continued to grow since then.

Alaska has been good to my family and me, and we have had many adventures. My oldest sister and others have asked me to put my stories into print so that people could see what life in Alaska was like when we arrived here. Over these past forty-two years we have had many unique experiences, some of which are almost unbelievable. Some of them probably should have been told before now, but at the time we didn't think anyone would be interested. I have always been an outdoors man, and I wanted to experience all that Alaska had to offer. My work schedule of working one week and being off the next week has provided me with plenty of opportunity to do what I love most.

Alaska was full of interesting people whom I have had the good fortune of knowing. Most of them are gone now, but I will never forget them, and I will always be grateful to them for their friendship and advice.

It may be worth mentioning here that Alaska can be a very dangerous place for the unwary. The weather can change quickly and is unpredictable. There are large animals in Alaska that are just as unpredictable as the weather, and you never know what they may or may not do. Then there is the element of surprise that can catch you even when you think you are prepared.

It didn't take me long to realize that living in Alaska would be different from anywhere else I have lived. It was a totally different life style from what I had been used to. I'd lived in areas where there is snow and ice, but Alaska's weather is more extreme than any place I'd ever been. After a while I began to realize in my heart that this is where I was meant to be.

It seemed to me like there were only two seasons in Alaska: winter and summer. The winters are eight months long, and it's dark most of the time. Starting in June the days get shorter and shorter until the sun is up for only a few hours a day. There are plenty of activities and many ways to enjoy the winter months in Alaska. But great care must be taken when you're out in it. The temperatures can range from minus 50 degrees to plus 40 degrees during these winters, and it can change rapidly. The lakes freeze over, but we've always used great care before going out on them.

My family and I have always enjoyed riding snow machines and ice fishing. Snow machines are a great way to explore Alaska because you can reach remote areas with relative ease. These activities helped to shorten the long winter months.

Another thing that takes time to get used to is driving on Alaska's roads during the winter. I've only had one driving accident since coming to Alaska, and that was caused by black ice. Black ice is a condition that occurs when the sun melts snow on the highway, and it refreezes again during the night. It's hard to see and is very slick.

In this accident I was taking my truck out of four-wheel drive while driving to Soldotna. When I pulled the lever to take the truck out of four-wheel drive I knew instantly that I had made a mistake. The truck went into a skid to the left. When I compensated for it the truck started to straighten out; then I realized I had overdone it, and the truck left the road at about a 45-degree angle. It was 20 degrees below zero that morning, and the snow that had been plowed was about three feet high along the shoulder of the road. It had frozen and was as hard as any brick wall.

I had my snowplow on the truck at the time, and when it hit the snow on the shoulder of the road it flipped end over end, landing on the passenger's side. I wasn't hurt, but it certainly disorientated me for a while. The truck was in a lot worse shape than I was it was a total wreck. It's hard to believe I came out of it with just a few bruises.

Later my oldest daughter told me that I must have had an angel on both of my shoulders. She must be right because I've come through a lot situations that could have maimed or killed me but didn't.

Spring breakup starts in April and is a welcomed relief from the darkness and the cold. I always start to perk up at this time of year.

The Alaskan summers can be beautiful, but there's always the rain to contend with, and I don't want to forget the mosquitoes. They aren't as bothersome on the Kenai Peninsula as they are in the northern parts of the state, but they can be unpleasant wherever they are.

The days are longer during the summer, and for a couple of months it will be daylight for most of the day. Winter or summer, Alaska is the most rugged and beautiful place I have ever seen, and I think that's why I'm still here.

Part One
Working in Alaska

The jobs I have worked at in Alaska have been varying and interesting. All of them have had times of quiet and episodes of excitement. Most of these episodes were adventures in themselves. I have chosen to relate some of these incidents so that you can see what working in Alaska was like for me. I haven't told all of them, only those that stand out in my memory as having been more extreme than others. God has truly had his hand on me, or I would not have survived many of these extremely dangerous situations.

I have worked at four jobs since coming to Alaska. The first one was with an oil-field service company where I was a laborer. I held this job until the work they were doing was finished. The work consisted of installing heater treatment units and piping on a Cook Inlet beach for Shell Oil Company. These units were for heating oil and removing water prior to the oil being put into large storage tanks.

Getting to the job was difficult because the roads north of Kenai were not paved. In fact there weren't many roads that were paved in 1965.

The job site was twelve miles north of Kenai, and we had to be pulled out of several mud holes encountered along the way. The oil companies had stationed small-tracked vehicles at the worst mud holes for this purpose.

On one particular day the wind came up, and we were not able to work. The wind was gusting to ninety miles an hour, and there were sheets of plywood and sheet metal flying all over the countryside. We had taken shelter in a building that was partly underground, so we were safe from the worst of it.

The barge that was laying the pipeline from a platform located in Cook Inlet broke loose from its moorings and the pipe they had been laying. When it was all over, the barge had washed up onto the beach. It took several weeks to get that barge back into the water and working again. Thankfully no one was hurt. This job lasted from October 1965 through January of 1966.

My next job was with Santa Fe drilling company on the Grayling Platform located out in Cook Inlet, about six miles off shore. Helicopters were used to ferry us to and from the platform. I was what they called a roustabout, which is the same thing as a laborer. I really didn't like this job because it was offshore, and when I wasn't working, I could see the town and car lights on the roads.

Sometimes the weather was bad, and the helicopters couldn't fly. So we were stuck on the platform until a tug could come out to take us in. Cook Inlet has one of the largest and fastest tide changes in the world. These changes can be as much as twenty feet or more from low tide to high tide. Add to that the wind, snow, and ice on Cook Inlet. This ice can be several miles long. Getting on that tug was quite an experience. They had to lower us to the tug in a personnel basket using a crane. It was sixty to eighty feet from the deck of the platform down to the tug. When one of these large pans of ice hit the legs of the platform, it would shake violently and sway back and forth until the ice had passed. The tug would get behind the platform legs and most of the time would be okay until the ice had passed. Sometimes the tug would get caught by the ice, and it would be pushed down the inlet for miles before it could work its way back through the ice to the platform. The tugs would take us to Arnes dock, where we would get off and arrange transportation to our vehicles that were parked at the helicopter port.

Arnes dock consisted of two or three World War II liberty ships that had been sunk to form a breakwater for the loading areas and boat ramps. The ice on Cook Inlet could be really bad at times, and I have actually been knocked out of my bunk when the ice hit the platform legs.

On one occasion we were unloading a large tug carrying a load of nine-inch-by-thirty-foot-long pieces of pipe, commonly known as casing. Each one of these joints of pipe weighed somewhere between four and six hundred pounds. We were stacking the pipe on the top deck of the platform when an ice flow hit the platform legs. The pipe shifted, and nine or ten joints rolled over the side. I still don't know how that pipe missed the tug, but thankfully it did. However the platform wasn't so lucky. When I looked over the side all of the ladders, landings, and doors that had been left open on that side of the platform were gone.

This kind of thing was not common, but on several other occasions we lost things over the side. Sometimes the items we were unloading would hit the tug. But as far as I know no one was ever hurt by these falling objects. If the tugs were damaged I never knew about it. I worked for Santa Fe drilling company from January 1966 through June of 1966.

The next job I had was with Coastal Drilling Company. I worked for them from late June 1966 thru June of 1970. Coastal had six complete land-based oil drilling rigs with all of their components. They had two very large buildings situated on five acres of land located in Soldotna. In one of these buildings they had a complete machine shop, including welding facilities. The second building was a mechanics shop where all of the various engines and vehicles were maintained and repaired. They could repair almost anything, and if they couldn't find parts they simply made them in the machine shop. I think Coastal Drilling was the largest employer in Soldotna at the time.

My first assignment with Coastal was working on one of these rigs in the Beaver Creek and Swanson River Fields. The Swanson River

Oil Field was operated by Standard Oil Company, and the Beaver Creek Field was operated by Marathon Oil Company. We also drilled oil and gas wells for Union Oil Company in the Kalifornski Field and other places around Alaska. Later we drilled wells for Texaco and Exxon.

During the winter of 1966 we were working on a rig for Marathon in the Beaver Creek field. The temperature was thirty-five below zero, and I was working the night shift. One night the driller sent me to the tool shed to get a tool. On my way to the tool shed I heard a strange sound and felt the ground start to vibrate. When I looked back at the rig I saw everyone running away from it. As they ran by me they were all shouting for me to run, which I did as fast as I could.

When we were a safe distance away from the rig what we saw was the most amazing thing I had ever seen. The drilling pipe was coming up out of the ground and breaking into long sections. Some of them were ninety feet long; others were much longer. This pipe was actually sticking into the frozen ground. All of this had started because we had drilled into a pocket of gas that was at an extremely high pressure. The driller had closed the blowout preventer equipment before he left the rig, but his actions didn't have the desired effect. It's hard to imagine what would have happened if he had not closed those hydraulic valves. The men who were on the rig certainly would not have had enough time to get off. We found out later that the blowout equipment had worked, but the gas had blown out from under it, on the wellhead pipe.

The noise was deafening; metal was screeching. The escaping gas was roaring, and the rocks, mud, and pipe coming out of the well head were banging off of everything. One thing we were all thankful for was that the gas did not ignite, and there was no fire. After the derrick collapsed, the lights on the rig went out. We couldn't see what was happening so we went to our vehicles to keep warm and have a little light. Our vehicles were parked outside of the drilling area to keep them from getting drilling mud all over them. It's a good thing they were, or we would have lost all of them.

The next morning when it got light enough to see what we observed was truly amazing. The rig was completely buried under a mound of mud and rock. This mound of mud and rocks looked like the small version of a volcano. The gas was still coming out of the well head, and it was still roaring.

We decided that there was nothing we could do until the gas flow either slowed down or stopped. So we posted one man with a radio to keep watch and inform the office if there were any changes. The rest of us went back to town until the company could decide what to do. We were sent home around five in the afternoon.

A few days later the company called and asked me to come in to the office; the drilling superintendent wanted to see me. He told me that he wanted me to work in the yard full time. My assignment was to make sure that all of the working rigs had everything they needed to continue working without interruption. This assignment meant I would be cleaning the equipment that was sent in from the rigs and making sure it was repaired and painted before it was put away. Four young men were assigned to me to help in accomplishing these tasks.

Whenever one of the operating rigs needed equipment we made arrangements with a local trucking company to take it out to them. Some of these loads weighed in excess of thirty thousand pounds. If a load sent to a rig was below two and a half tons we hauled it out on our own trucks. There were three trucking companies in the area, Arctic Motor Freight, Homer Freight lines, and Tachick Motor Freight. Homer Freight Lines had trucks especially designed to move heavy oil-field equipment, so we used them most of the time.

Three weeks after the blowout the gas had subsided enough for us to begin the cleanup and recovery of the rig. Homer Freight Line brought out four large wench trucks, several very large bull dozers, and two cranes. It was a tough job to dig out and transport all of that equipment to the yard, especially since it was still thirty-five below zero, and the mound of dirt on top of it was still frozen. We didn't think it was possible but eventually it was done, and the site was cleaned up.

Somehow the welders installed a valve on the wellhead and closed it, shutting off the flow of gas. We restored the drilling site as close to its original condition as we could. We were conscious of the environment and did everything we could to keep it clean.

When the wreckage from this rig was brought in to the yard we proceeded with the clean up and repairs, where it was possible. The equipment that was directly impinged on by the gas coming out of the wellhead was beyond recovery. It was cleaned up and disposed of. The bent pipe we recovered was stacked in the back of the yard; we would straighten it later. That entire rig was cleaned, repaired, and returned to service in about six months.

Blowouts are not a common occurrence on drilling rigs, but they do happen. During the time I worked for Coastal we had another rig experience a blowout, but we were able to stop it before it got out of control.

I mentioned earlier that we delivered some of the equipment needed on the rigs with our own trucks. Some of these trips were memorable because of what happened along the way. Most of the time these rigs were not on the road system, so getting to them was not easy. Some of our drilling took place hundreds of miles from our home base.

On one of these trips another man and I loaded a two-and-a-half-ton flatbed truck with a heavy load, a little over three thousand pounds. We made sure the load was chained down and ready for the long drive. This load was going to the Beluga Field located on the other side of Cook Inlet. To get there we would have to go through Anchorage, Palmer, and Wasilla. The distance to Wasilla from Soldotna is one hundred eighty eight miles. Wasilla was a very small community, and there wasn't much there. At Wasilla we turned left on a gravel road headed to a place called Houston. When we arrived at what we thought was the road going to the rig we made another left turn. It was snowing, and the temperature was twenty below zero, and it was dark. This road was very rough, and we had to move slowly so our load wouldn't shift on us. We started up a steep incline, and I mentioned to Mark that we were going to have to put the chains on pretty soon. We made it to the top, and immediately the road started down a very steep grade. I slammed on the brakes, but they didn't help. We slid all the way to the bottom and out onto a lake. The truck spun around at least twice before coming to a stop. The ice on the lake was free of snow. Apparently the wind had kept it off of this part of the lake. It's hard to believe we didn't break through that ice. We knew we were going to have to put the chains on to get back up that steep incline.

Once the chains were laid out in front of the rear wheels I got into the cab and began moving the truck forward onto the chains. After I had moved the truck about three feet I got out and looked under the truck to see if it needed to be moved again. That's when I saw someone standing behind Mark. He was kneeling under the truck adjusting the chains. When the man spoke Mark rose up quickly striking his head on the truck. It almost knocked him out. When I got around the truck to where they were the man was helping Mark up. I told him we weren't expecting to see anyone this far off of the main road in the middle of the night. He told me he was here because of a trap line he was running in the area, and he wasn't expecting anyone either. The man had a small cabin built off of the trail, and when he heard us drive by he came out to see what was going on. When we had the chains on we went back to the main road and got on the right trail to the rig. After the supplies had been delivered we returned to Soldotna without any other problems.

The company purchased a larger truck for deliveries to the rigs in 1968. It was a Peterbilt tractor with a wench on the back and had a forty-foot flatbed trailer. It would haul thirty-five thousand pounds of freight so we didn't have to make as many trips to the rigs. I was very happy we didn't have this truck when we slid out onto that lake.

Most of the time we think of our jobs as being boring and somewhat repetitious. This was not so with Coastal Drilling Company. I was able to learn and progress to a new level while employed there, thanks in no small part to the people I worked with.

One fine day in May the drilling superintendent asked me to burn the trash. This trash came from six trailers where the drilling pushers and maintenance supervisors lived with their families. There was trash generated in the shops and offices of the company as well as things like pallets, broken lumber, paper, and metal shavings from the lathes. We had a very large pit that was used as a dump There were no dumps in Soldotna at the time. It was forty feet long, thirty feet wide, and about thirty feet deep and would hold a lot of trash. There was a wooden platform built on one end of this pit where we steam cleaned cosmolene off of new engines.

I had burned this trash several times without any problem. But on this occasion it would be different. In May here in Alaska it is spring break-up. This is the time of year when the snow is melting, and the frozen ground starts to thaw. There was still some snow on the ground, and the trash in the pit was wet. There were six new G.M.C. diesel engines on the cleaning platform waiting to be cleaned. I went and filled a gallon jug with a mixture of gasoline and diesel to use as a starter. When I lit the gasoline and diesel mixture I heard a satisfying whoomp, and the trash started to burn. As I walked away there was a secondary whoomp that I had not expected. The fire started to accelerate, and was soon a very large fire. Oily black smoke with red and yellow flames running through it was at least a hundred feet high and climbing. It didn't take long for the Soldotna and Kenai volunteer fire departments to get here. Apparently they had received calls from several residents who thought Soldotna was burning down. The fire burned all day and into the night. We lost the cleaning dock and all of those new engines. The metal on the mechanics shop which was about forty feet from the dump was buckled, but thankfully it didn't catch fire. The dump was still smoking when I came in to work the next morning, but everything in it had been burned, including the new engines. We were able to locate the reason for this excessive fire the next day. A ten-thousand-gallon diesel fuel tank had been delivered to the yard from one of the rigs a few months earlier. When it was unloaded in the yard the four-inch valve on the outlet of the tank was damaged, and the diesel that was left in the tank had leaked out. It had found its way into the trash dump in a ditch running under the ice and snow. I don't know how much diesel was in the tank, but it had to be a lot for that fire to burn as long as it did and be as intense as it was.

Not long after this incident the company promoted me to yard foreman. I was placed under the supervision of the mechanics supervisor, Matt Humeky, Mark's dad. Matt was a fine man, and I was able to learn a great deal from him. He was the best supervisor I have ever worked for in all of my working years.

In the summer of 1967 Soldotna became a first-class city. There was a parade, and everyone was celebrating and having a good time.

The company decided to throw a party and asked me to clean up the mechanics shop so they could have it there. My boss asked me to tend bar for them because I didn't drink. I explained to him that I didn't know how to mix drinks. He said, "Don't worry about that; we'll tell you how we want them made," so I agreed to do it. This turned out to be a mistake for me. It all started out okay, but the more these fellows drank the wilder the party got. At one point they were lighting large fire crackers. I think they were called "cherry bombs." They were throwing them at the ventilation fans located above our heads. When the blades of the fans hit these fire crackers they would be deflected back down into the crowd and explode. No one was hurt, but it was dangerous, and I felt like it shouldn't have been done. After this they filled a very large weather balloon with acetylene. They took it outside, tied a burning rag to it, and let it go. When the balloon was about two hundred feet up it exploded. I think that explosion could have been heard for miles; it was very loud, and we all felt the concussion produced by it.

One of the peculiar things that was going on was that a lot of these people were bringing their drinks back to me and complaining about the taste. I would explain that I wasn't a bartender, to which they would say, "Well, taste it." When I explained that I wouldn't know what they were supposed to taste like, they would show me what they wanted me to do to their drink, and then they would say, "Taste it now, and you'll know the next time."

After this had happened over a period of several hours I didn't care anymore, and I was drinking Segrams seven straight out of the bottle. About this time my wife came in and figured out that I was very drunk. She reached out and took hold of my ear and literally dragged me out of the party. She took me home where I became very, very sick. I suffered from the effects of this drinking binge for several days. I found out later that this had been planed by some of the supervisors before the party had even started. They laughed about how my feet weren't even on the ground when my wife pulled me out of there. Matt apologized to me later; he said they didn't realize my wife would get so upset. He also thought it was one of the funniest exits he had ever seen.

In the early fall of 1967 we moved our trailer to land we had purchased six miles south of Soldotna. The trailer was a ten-by-fifty-five Marlette mobile home. My father-in-law and I built a septic system and set the trailer up on cement and concrete blocks. The water well had already been drilled, so we hooked it up along with the power lines that had been run to the trailer by the local utility company. We also built a lean-to on one side of the trailer that was to be used as a master bedroom. A lot of people were living in trailers when we arrived here.

One morning when I was driving to work I was stopped just before getting to the bridge that crosses the Kenai River. The police officer who stopped me said they were only allowing one car at a time on the bridge because of ice that had backed up against it. Apparently an ice dam on a glacial lake located high up in the mountains above Kenai Lake had failed, sending a huge amount of water and ice down the river. This huge flow of water had broken up the ice on Kenai Lake and the river. When the ice got down to the bridge it was backed up and had formed an effective dam. I could have stood flat footed in the middle of the bridge and touched the ice with my fingers without bending over. The bridge was about forty feet above the water in the river. Anyone who lived south of the bridge would not be able to get to Soldotna if the bridge collapsed. It was a tense situation and lasted for several days. Most of the people who lived north of the river were okay, except for some who lived on Rebel Run Road and a few other roads that were in low-lying areas along the river!

We visited one of our friends who lived in one of these areas to see if we could help them. Their double-wide trailer had been flooded, and the water inside had frozen. When we were able to get the doors open there was four feet if ice inside of their home. We could see some of their furniture frozen in the ice. The people and businesses in Soldotna were wonderful; everyone pitched in and helped these folks.

A little later that fall we were moving drilling pipe to the pipe racks located next to the machine shop. We had five fork lifts of varying size for loading and moving drilling equipment around the yard. On this occasion the operator had five or six thirty-foot-long-by-five-inch pieces of drilling pipe on the forks. These pipes weighed somewhere around four hundred pounds apiece. One of the pipes fell off, and he was pushing it along the ground trying to get it back on the forks.

What I did next I had done many times before. I stopped him and walked around to the front of the fork lift and put my foot on the pipe he had dropped. When he started to move forward to retrieve it his foot slipped off of the brake and onto the gas pedal. When the forklift lunged forward he immediately slammed on the brakes, but it was too late. The pipe rolled off of the forks. One of them landed on my right ankle; the others had turned at an angle and were on top of the one that had me pinned down. I was on my knees and my ankle was bent at an impossible angle. Someone had brought up another fork lift and had raised the pipe enough for me to get my leg out from under it. It turned out that my ankle was broken in several places. I was flown to a hospital in Anchorage where they took me into surgery to repair the damage. There were no hospitals on the Kenai Peninsula at the time.

This was the first work-related accident I had ever had, and I have never had another one; however, there have been many near misses.

My boss told me in late spring of 1968, that we were going to prepare one of our rigs to be shipped to Fairbanks. He said that it would require special attention because it was going to be flown from Fairbanks to what he called the North Slope. He also stated we were going to have to make steel parts for the top of large posts that were being set in the permafrost. The rig would sit on top of these posts and be welded to the parts we had fabricated to protect the permafrost. When we received the instructions from the airline on how they wanted the rig packaged to fit into the planes the instructions included the size and weight limits of each load to be shipped. It turned out that some of the rig would have to be cut into smaller sections. Once the rig arrived at the North Slope it would be reassembled and set up on the spot where it would begin drilling.

This was the largest job that Coastal Drilling had ever attempted during the time I was employed with them. As I recall the bins we made were thirty-two feet long, eight feet wide, and six feet high. They were constructed out of heavy, eight-inch eye beams and four-inch channel iron welded together.

These bins would hold the drilling pipe, collars, and smaller items that were to be shipped. Most of the rig components could be shipped as they were, because they met the size and weight limits and were self contained. However, we did place smaller parts inside of these self-contained units where space was available. Arctic Motor Freight was the trucking company we used. I think there were eighty-seven loads hauled over the highway to Fairbanks. The rig went into operation in the summer of 1968.

I'm not sure if this was the first drilling rig on the North Slope, but it was among one of the first ones.

Early that fall we received a communication from the rig up north. They said the blowout equipment had malfunctioned and had closed on the drill pipe while they were drilling. This had twisted the pipe off, and it had fallen down into the well they were drilling. When this happens they have to use what is called fishing tools to retrieve the drill pipe and bring it back up to the drilling floor where it can be repaired. The company sent me to the rig to see if I could determine what had caused the blowout equipment to close without being activated.

I flew to Fairbanks on a commercial airliner. After spending the night in the company's apartment, the company's expediter in Fairbanks booked me a flight to the North Slope on a twin otter. This airplane was owned and operated by a local charter company. The flight took several hours and was pretty rough, due to a high wind that was blowing.

When we arrived at the rig site I noticed that there were no other rigs in this particular area. The camp was rather large; it had sleeping trailers, cooking and eating facilities, and other buildings I couldn't identify. Once on the ground I started walking to the camp, and the plane took off for its return flight. I think these pilots were show offs because they flew around the derrick a couple of times. On one of these passes the plane's engines changed pitch, and the plane began to slow down. It actually came to a complete stop in mid-air, and the wind was slowly pushing it backwards. After this stunt the engines changed pitch again, and the plane flew off towards Fairbanks. This is the only time I have ever seen an airplane back up while it was flying. I know this is hard to believe, but it actually happened, just as I have stated.

Alaska's North Slope is an area that is largely unpopulated. The ground here is frozen year round and is referred to as permafrost. It is barren ground without trees or brush. Most of it in the area where I went was pretty flat.

I spent three days at the rig looking for the problem that had brought me here. We found the problem on the third day, when the driller and I traced the hydraulic lines to the accumulator shed. One of the automatic valves located here was communicating from one port to another. This valve is the one that supplies hydraulic fluid to the blowout equipment. It is activated when the driller throws a switch located at his station on the drilling floor. We replaced the faulty valve, and there were no further problems. This was the first time I had ever been to the north slope of Alaska, and I never got up there again. The same plane returned and took me back to Fairbanks. From here I flew back to Soldotna.

My father-in-law and his family left Alaska in September of 1968. He had been transferred to Groveland, Florida, to pastor a church there.

The owners of Coastal Drilling sold the company to Parker Drilling in the late summer of 1969. Parker Drilling Company's main base of operations was in California. As soon as the new drilling superintendent arrived he started implementing changes to our operations, immediately. It was apparent to me that some of these changes were going to have a negative effect on our drilling operations, especially during the harsh Alaskan winters.

Many of the old supervisors were being replaced, and I was removed from my position as yard foreman. I was told that it was an unnecessary position, and I was reassigned to work in the machine shop. The feeling of working with family was gone, and I knew I wouldn't be able to work for this company much longer.

I had worked in the machine shop off and on for a long time. A year or so earlier I had made some parts for a chemical plant that was being built north of Kenai. When I delivered these parts I discovered that this was going to be a very large plant. The warehouse I was directed to was one of the largest buildings on the site. On my way out of the plant area I stopped in at the office and asked if they were hiring. They told me that they didn't have any openings at the time but asked me to check back later.

In May of 1970 I was delivering parts to another company north of Kenai. Since I was in the area I stopped in at the offices of the newly completed chemical plant to see if they were hiring. This time they made me an appointment to meet with their personnel manager.

In late May I returned for the scheduled interview. I was told by the lady at the front desk that he was unavailable. After hearing this I asked her to tell him that if he didn't want to see me then he should at least have the courtesy of telling me himself.

At this point he stepped around the corner and invited me to his office for the interview.

He asked me about my military and work record then gave me a piece of paper with fifteen questions on it. I was told that this was a test he gave to everyone who applied for work with the company. He told me to answer as many of them as I could in fifteen minutes. The questions were multiple choice. I answered twelve of them and left three of them blank. When he returned he asked me why I hadn't answered all of the questions on the test. I explained to him that I didn't know the answers and rather than guess, I had left them blank. Apparently he liked my answer because he told me I was hired. As I was leaving he told me it would be okay if I wanted to give the company I was working for a two-week notice before leaving them, which I did.

I left Parker Drilling Company on June, 15, 1970, to go to work for Collier Carbon and Chemical Company. This was the company that operated the plant. The plant had been built by Union Oil Company and Mitsubishi Gas, a Japanese-owned company. Union Oil owned sixty percent, and Mitsubishi Gas owned the remaining forty percent. This was a large plant and consisted of an ammonia, urea, and utility plant. It also had maintenance shops consisting of seven different crafts. These were machinists, mechanics, electricians, instrument technicians, insulators, welders, and laborers. Management was located in the front office with the engineers, fire and safety, and chemists. I think there were around one hundred fifty employees working here at the time.

Ammonia and urea are used all over the world as fertilizer, but these products have many other uses. I was given an introduction class and assigned as a low-level operator in the urea plant. On my first day in this plant I was intimidated by its size and the obvious sophistication of the instrumentation that controlled it. The operators who had been here since the plant started were to train the new operators. I think the plants had been in operation for about eight months then. The control rooms were located close to the center of each plant at ground level. There were five operators on each shift and one unit coordinator. All of the operators wore radios with head sets and were equipped with a small valve wrench and a pair of pliers. When we were out in the operating areas we were in constant communication with the control rooms.

The urea plant produced one thousand tons of urea a day. The product was stored in a huge warehouse until it could be shipped. The company had built a loading wharf out into Cook Inlet and it was located about three-quarters of a mile off shore. It had a narrow tunnel built out to it from the plant. The wharf's loading building was built on top of eight large pilings that had been set deep into the bottom of Cook Inlet. The pilings they used were at least twenty feet across the top, and they had been filled with concrete. There were six more pilings of the same size set to the left and right of the loading building. Catwalks were built from the landing of the wharf building to these pilings. On top of each piling they had placed pelican hooks and line wenches to accommodate the lines running from the ships. This loading facility was approximately three hundred feet long.

All of the products produced in the plants were sent to this wharf via pipe and conveyor belt, where it was loaded onto ships. Everyone participated in the loading of these ships. During the winter the ice in Cook Inlet was a problem, and loading had to be shut down frequently.

There were two large front-end loaders in the urea warehouse. These were used to move the urea to the conveyor belts located in the center of the building, under the floor. One of these loaders had a twenty-yard bucket and was the largest front-end loader in the state at the time. The tires on this loader were ten feet tall and four feet wide.

The warehouse where the urea was stored was as large as a football field; it was partially underground, and the lower section was made out of concrete. These concrete walls were about twenty feet high and three feet thick. There were large overhead doors at each end. The rest of the building was made out of galvanized metal that sat on top of the concrete walls. The roof at the center of the building was about ninety feet high. There was a conveyor belt located at the top of the warehouse that brought the urea here from the plant and distributes it evenly.

One night I was operating the large loader pushing urea onto the conveyor. The urea was not flowing like it was supposed to, and a cliff face started to develop. It was about sixty feet high. I was attempting to break it up when it suddenly collapsed and buried the loader. The windshield was pushed back into the cab, and it pinned me in the seat. Urea filled the cab up to my neck. Because of the windshield and urea I couldn't reach the controls to back up. The cliff I was trying to knock down looked like it was going to break off again when the operator who was running the other loader had seen the urea cave in and bury my loader. He started removing the urea from behind my loader and attached a chain to pull me out. Shortly after he pulled me out the rest of the cliff fell.

After this incident we had the company build a machine that was capable of bringing down these cliffs from a distance. We didn't have any more problems with burying loaders after the new machine went into service. I spent a year in the urea plant, and in June of 1971 I was transferred to the ammonia plant.

The primary difference between these plants is that urea is a solid, and ammonia is a liquid. Ammonia is made out of nitrogen and hydrogen. Urea is made from ammonia and CO_2. The ammonia plant was producing around one thousand tons a day. Some of this was sent to the urea plant, and the remainder was put into a large storage tank prior to shipping. This plant was just as intimidating as the urea plant had been. I was again trained by the senor operators on shift. After about six months of training we were allowed to work an area. There were seven operators and one unit coordinator on each shift in this plant. There were four shifts. This plant had two extra operators because the boiler house, generators, and the equipment located there were operated by this plant. There were numerous plant shut downs caused by various things during the first few years of operation, and it could be very exciting indeed. If you've ever seen the movie, *The China Syndrome*, you will have an idea of what a plant shutdown can be like.

On one of my night shifts I was up on a large vessel changing the valves around to balance the flow. I was on the second level, about twenty feet high. The valve wrench I was using slipped off of the valve wheel, and I fell down through the pipes. I hit the ground on my back and was barely conscious. This was another near-miss accident. It's what happened after this incident that I have never been able to forget or explain to myself or anyone else.

While I was lying there someone called me over the radio and informed me I had an emergency phone call in the control room. I don't know why but I immediately thought about my brother. He was a Navy pilot stationed at Norfolk, Virginia. Somehow I knew what had happened, and I really dreaded taking that call. When I picked up the telephone my oldest sister's husband confirmed my worst fears and related to me every thing that he knew about what had happened.

Apparently my brother Tom and five other officers were doing tests on a new plane. It was one of the Navy's surveillance aircraft. It was an E-2B Hawkeye. They had just taken off for a flight to New York, and on the way they would be conducting tests on the electronics equipment. Witnesses said that just after takeoff the plane began to sputter and loose altitude. They said that the plane veered out over Chesapeake Bay and crashed about fifty yards offshore. It hit the water at a seventy-degree angle. I found out later that the plane had struck the water at around five hundred miles an hour, and the water at the crash site was about forty feet deep. I was told that the largest piece of the plane after it had been recovered was the nose wheel.

The company gave me funeral leave to attend his funeral, which would be held in Denver, Colorado. My wife was about eight months along in her pregnancy with our third child, and her doctor said she shouldn't be flying. After I returned from the funeral my wife gave birth to our son. We named him after my brother. His name would be Arthur Thomas Dunn.

It was around this time that Unocal bought out Mitsubishi Gas. It now controlled the entire complex. The operations of the plant would now be taken over by Union Oil and Collier Carbon, and Chemical was let go. Unocal made changes in the operations department right away. They assigned one operator from each shift to work in the generator building and another one to the boiler house on a permanent basis. This would leave five operators and the unit coordinator in the ammonia plant.

My new assignment was in the boiler house. This boiler house contained three five-hundred-fifty-pound, gas-fired boilers. Each one of these boilers was capable of producing one hundred ten thousand pounds per hour of steam at six hundred degrees. There was a water system supplied from three large wells, all of which were located off site from the plant. This water had to be demineralized to prevent scale build up inside of the boiler tubes and inside of the steam turbines that used steam to drive them. The water from this system was put into a large storage tank and was supplied to the entire plant. We demineralized twelve hundred gallons of water per minute twenty four hours a day with this system. There were two large instrument air dryers which supplied dry air to all of the air-driven instruments located throughout the plants. The front of the boilers and all of this equipment was inside of a large building located at the north end of the ammonia plant.

A few years later Unocal decided to build another ammonia and urea plant here, north of the existing plants. The new urea plant would be a little different from the old one. It would produce urea granules instead of prills. It was a massive undertaking that took the better part of three years to complete. What we ended up with was one of the largest plants of this type in the world. The utility plant was the largest in-plant utility system in existence at that time. Everything was doubled and in some instances tripled. During the construction there were at least sixteen hundred men and women working around the clock. When construction was finished the company had at least five hundred full-time employees.

There was one fatality during the construction of the new plants. A young man twenty-two years old was directing a huge scraper outside of the utility plant. This scraper is the same kind you will see used on highway construction, moving large quantities of earth.

Apparently he was removing stakes from behind this machine when he stumbled and fell. The operator didn't see him and had continued backing up. He was run over by one of the rear tires. Our fire and safety people managed to keep him alive until an ambulance arrived to transport him to the hospital. I heard later that he had died in the ambulance on the way to the hospital. Fire and safety told me that every bone in his body had been broken.

Unocal changed the name of the plant to Union Chemicals. They also had to change the designation of the plants to eliminate confusion during normal operations. The old ammonia plant was called Plant One and the old urea plant was called Plant Two. The old section of the utility plant was called Plant Three and the new section was designated as Plant Six. The new ammonia plant was called Plant Four and the new urea plant was Plant Five. Plant Four and Five's control room was combined into one control room. The radio communications system had to be upgraded to one that had six frequencies. That way we could communicate with our operators in the field without interfering with the other plants.

The utility plant ended up with ten five-hundred-fifty-pound boilers capable of producing nine hundred thousand pounds of dry steam per hour. There were thirteen generators capable of producing twenty seven thousand kilowatts of power. This was enough electrical power to supply all of the communities on the Kenai Peninsula at this time. Our water systems produced twenty-six hundred gallons per minute of clean demineralized water. This required six large water wells to keep up with the demand.

They built us a control room with all of the latest instrumentation needed to control the plants. This utility plant became the nerve center of the entire complex. If we went down all of the plants usually went down with us.

Before the new plants could begin their start up the utility plant had to be reorganized and staffed. We would have to be in operation before they could begin purging their systems. I was promoted to unit coordinator on one of the shifts. This was a salaried position, and I had five operators on my shift. There were five areas of operations in the utility plant that required constant surveillance. For startup we worked double shifts; there was plenty of excitement during the start up.

The first thing we did was to get one of the boilers lit and on line. Once that had been accomplished we had to blow steam through all the pipes in the plant to clean them out. This is a touchy procedure because some of the lines contained water left over from pressure testing. When you put six-hundred-degree steam into a line containing water, the water will expand sixteen hundred times its original volume. The line will jump and hammer, flanges will separate, and in some instances the pipe will rupture. So the steam had to be introduced into these lines very slowly until the water had flashed into steam and the line was hot.

During any new construction there is dirt, welding slag, and all manner of junk in the pipes. We actually found coke cans, and on one occasion an eight-ton "come along" inside of these pipes. A come along is a hand-operated wench with cables and has a hook located on each end. When we were able to get it out of the pipe it was as shiny as a new silver coin.

There are thousands of miles of pipe in these plants, ranging in sizes from one-quarter of an inch up to thirty-six inches in diameter. All of this pipe and their related vessels had to be insulated against the extreme cold that can occur during an Alaskan winter. Blowing these pipes out with steam was a formidable job, and it took eight weeks to accomplish. When we were satisfied that the pipes were clean the start-up of our plant proceeded. Within six month and after many setbacks we had the utility plant up and running.

Once we were running smoothly we started supplying the new ammonia and urea plants with what they needed to proceed with their startup. It took them the better part of a year to start making product. They were held at a lower rate of production until all of the bugs in their plants were worked out.

While all of this was going on the company decided that we needed a loading crew at the wharf. They appointed a wharf coordinator on each shift and gave him five operators to accomplish his task. Their area of responsibility started at the large urea warehouses. It also included four front-end loaders and all of the conveyor belts from there to the wharf. They reported to the utility plant coordinators who kept up with the shipping schedules and staffing of the wharf during loading. It was our responsibility to call operators out for overtime when it became necessary, in our plant and at the wharf during loading.

One afternoon the wharf crew was in the process of loading a large ship with urea. This ship's capacity was twenty-five thousand tons, and it was half full. The ice on Cook Inlet was about a mile offshore, and the tide was starting to come in, but nobody seemed to be concerned with it. Later in the evening the wind shifted, and the ice came in towards the wharf.

Apparently no one noticed the change in the position of the ice until it was too late. When the ice started pushing against the ship it started moving, and some of the lines holding it in place started snapping. The captain started the ship's engines and attempted to hold the ship against the wharf. His actions did little to stop the ship from breaking loose from its moorings. All of the lines holding the ship had parted by now, and it was being pushed down the inlet. He was able to turn the ship and run it between two of the pilings. This effectively wedged the ship in and allowed the ice to slide along its side until it had passed. Eventually with the aid of tugs he was able to get out into the open water again. We couldn't tie him up to the wharf again because of the extensive damage we had sustained, so he left with his cargo holds half full.

One of our catwalks had been torn loose and fell into the water. The pilings he had gone between were bent in opposite directions. One of them was leaning towards shore, and the other one was leaning towards the open water. These pilings had been bent over by about thirty degrees. The weight and power of that ice was an awesome thing to behold.

It took the company three weeks to make temporary repairs so the wharf could resume operations. The repairs that were needed would have to wait until summer before they could be done. I never heard if the ship had sustained any damage, but I'm sure there had to be some. No one was hurt in this incident, and we were thankful for that.

The operation manuals for the wharf were rewritten, and the procedures for tying ships to the dock were strengthened. We still had a few near misses, but we never lost another ship due to the ice in Cook Inlet.

We handled all kinds of chemicals in these plants. They were used to control conductivity and other conditions that we needed to control in the process.

There was also the threat of fire because of the natural gas used and the hydrogen that was produced in the ammonia plants.

The fire and safety department was constantly training plant personnel in the use of full-cover suits and fire-fighting techniques. The company provided us with the bunker gear and Scott air packs used by all fire departments. This gear was kept in the plants so it would be readily available if it was needed. There were several instances that this training and equipment were put to use and paid off.

I think this is a good place to explain what happened in the control room when an incident occurred in any of these plants. In the control rooms there were alarm panels located above the controllers, charts, and gauges on the control-room board. These alarm panels were twelve inches high and thirty-six inches wide. Each one would contain around forty alarms, and there could be from twelve to twenty of them in each control room. The individual alarms in each panel were one inch by three inches. Alarms that were less severe would light up using white lights and sound an audible alarm. These alarms could be dealt with by an operator who went to the effected area and made an adjustment to the process or by the control room operator, who simply made an adjustment on the board.

It's the red alarms on these panels that would get your attention immediately. When the red lights appeared and there were audible sounds on the panel. It usually meant that a piece of equipment had tripped off line, blocking some part of the process. While it might seem like this was total pandemonium to someone who was not familiar with operations and the process, it was not. The only time it was pandemonium was when there was a fire, explosion, or rupture of some part of the process. At times like these all of the alarms would light up, and the operators would be running to and fro as the control room directed them. I have seen this kind of shut down go on for twelve hours until the plants were completely down or some kind of control was achieved.

During one such incident in Plant Two on one of the larger vessels they had a sight glass that was leaking. These sight glasses were very thick pieces of glass installed on the side of a vessel so that the operators could observe the level in the vessel. It was attached to a flange and has gaskets on both sides to keep it from leaking. This vessel had three sight glasses spaced about three feet apart; they were six-inch glasses. The center glass had developed a leak, and a work order had been written to have maintenance repair it.

When the maintenance man assigned to check the leak came in to the control room he was alone. Maintenance usually worked in pairs, and no one was allowed to perform work alone for safety reasons. He was informed about this policy and stated he didn't come to repair it. He said he was only going to look at it so he would know what tools they needed to make the repairs. An operator took him up to see the faulty sight glass. It was a small, wispy leak at the gasket. Apparently the operator received a call on his radio to make adjustments in his area and went off to take care of it. The man was only supposed to look at this leak.

This particular vessel is about fifty feet high and was kept at two hundred fifty pounds of pressure per square inch. The temperature inside of it was two hundred degrees, and it held a very large volume of material. Not long after they went out to look at the sight glass a loud roar was heard coming from the plant. The board operator informed the unit coordinator that he was losing pressure on this vessel. It took an hour for the operators to stabilize the plant enough so that some one could suit up and try to find him.

When they located him he was dead, and half of his face was gone. In the ensuing investigation it was determined that he had tried to tighten the flange on this sight glass with a pair of pliers, and it had blown out completely. This was the second death suffered in these plants, and thankfully it was the last.

As modern technology became available we incorporated it into the plants. The plants were constantly upgrading and improving in process and control. When computers were introduced into the plants everyone was required to attend school to learn how they worked. I had purchased an Apple computer and printer for my son to help him with his schooling, so I had a little experience on how they worked but it wasn't much. The Internet as we know it today was not available then. With computerized controls the plants were much easier to operate, and we experienced fewer plant shutdowns.

Unocal was really good about educating its work force. Over the years I have attended all manner of classes covering everything from management to specific pieces of machinery. I also completed several college exams on various subjects. These courses and exams were on physics and how to apply them in the workplace. I am grateful to Unocal for the education they made available to me. I have completed fifteen quality-control and management seminars and five college classes at the Kenai Peninsula College. This training was made available during my work weeks, and it still helps me today.

One thing comes to mind about how the physics of hydraulics can sometimes cause problems. We had large vessels that our water passed through to remove the iron and other metals. There were large manhole covers on the top of these vessels to permit entry for inspection and maintenance if it became necessary. Apparently the bolts that held this particular cover in place had rusted severely and had lost the ability to hold the cover in place. These vessels could process around six hundred gallons per minute when operating normally. There were fourteen of them in the plant.

It's amazing how much water can come out of these man holes when the lid is blown off. There was a twenty-four inch column of water shooting straight up into the air above the vessel. It was held at eighty pounds of pressure and was dumping the full well capacity of twelve hundred gallons per minute. The water went up about forty feet and blew the sheet metal off the roof of the building. Operators had to block in the manual inlet and outlet valves before we could get it under control and silence the alarms that were sounding off. What caused this to happen was an automatic valve controlling the flow out of these vessels had suddenly closed, and the pressure in the vessels had gone up to two hundred pounds instantly. The vessel with rusted bolts on the cover was not able to hold the higher pressure and failed. There were a lot of instances where things like this happened. But most of the time they didn't happen at the same time. The principles of cause and effect came into play here. The cause being a valve that failed: the direct effect was the lid being blown off of a vessel.

On one of my days off I received a call from the plant at two in the morning. I was informed that there had been an explosion at the plant, and they wanted everyone to report to work. When I arrived at the utility plant I saw that the old section had been totally destroyed. The Plant Three building had been blown apart, and nearly all of the equipment had sustained damage and would not run. All of the plants were knocked off line. Their vents were open, and the noise was unbelievable.

After we were able to isolate the old utility plant from the new utility plant we restarted the new utility section. Once we were stable the new urea and ammonia plants were started up and ran at a reduced rate. Through the use of inter ties we were able to get the old urea plant up and running also at reduced rates. All three of these plants were running at twenty-five percent of their normal capacity. Most of the damage was confined to the old ammonia plant and the old utility plant. It was apparent that it would be a long time before they'd be able operate again

The cause of the explosion was from a large storage tank located behind the old section of the utility plant. This tank was one hundred feet in diameter and twenty-five feet high. It contained byproducts produced by the ammonia plants that were stored here until they could be disposed of. After the investigation we learned what had caused the tank to explode.

Someone had gone up to the top of the tank and looked in to see where the level was and had failed to close the cover when he came back down. The content of this tank is a mixture of ammonia, hydrogen, and the liquid used to carry it through the process. The level in the tank at the time of the explosion was around three feet. When this liquid is under pressure it will not release the gasses it is carrying. But at normal atmospheric pressure the gasses will be released.

It takes three things to start a fire or cause an explosion: one is air, another is fuel, and the third is a heat source. The fuel and air mixture coming out of the tank must have been at the proper mixture, and when a nearby electric motor started it provided the heat for ignition from a spark caused by faulty brushes. No one was injured in this incident, but it cost the company millions of dollars to repair and clean up the mess left by the explosion.

Sometimes we would be caught completely by surprise when something happened. My operators and I were sitting in the control room one evening when a red alarm sounded. It was telling us that the feed water pump that supplied water to five of our boilers had tripped off, and no water was going to the boilers. This is about the worst thing that can happen in our plant excluding a power outage. When the operator tried to start the electric-driven back-up, he found a maintenance tag on it, and it couldn't be started. The steam-driven pump wouldn't restart, and he informed us that the whole building was shaking and moving. We informed the process plants, and they started reducing rates and starting up electric-driven back-up equipment, realizing that we were going to loose half of our normal steam capacity. The operator opened the vents on the five boilers that lost their water supply, and they started depressuring. The board operator cut the gas to these boilers so they wouldn't overheat. The vessel where the pumps got their water from had filled up and was dumping and venting. This vessel was on the third story of the building and was forty feet long and forty feet around. It had a smaller vessel mounted on top of it that stripped oxygen out of the water using fifty-pound steam before it reached the boilers. Normally there is eighty pounds of pressure on this vessel, and the water in it is held at two hundred fifty degrees. When the pressure dropped due to the vents opening all of this water was flashing into steam. The main vent dumped directly into the plant effluent system. This was a twelve-foot-diameter, buried cement pipe running the entire length of the plants. It was three-quarters of a mile long. The effluent water in this line came from various places, such as wash-down water, water seals on the pumps, and building floor drains. There was a manhole cover every three hundred feet along this line. When the steam from this vent went into the effluent line it flashed all of the water contained in it to steam. This expansion caused all of the manhole covers to be blown off of the line.

We weren't aware of this until one of the plants called and told us it had happened. The effluent system was severely damaged and took months to repair.

In Alaska we sometimes experienced earthquakes. Most of them were remote and caused little damage. There were a few of them that were close and strong enough to rattle dishes and scare us. But there wasn't much damage caused by them.

We have had two volcanic eruptions, and there was cause for concern when they happened. The first one was on Augustine Island located on the other side of Cook Inlet. This island is situated across from Homer, Alaska, about seventy-five miles away.

It erupted in late March, 1986, and lasted for about five months. When the wind was in our direction we would get ash all over our house and cars. I had to change the breather filters in our cars and keep the ash washed off of them. When we were outside we had to wear masks to keep from breathing it. This eruption didn't have much effect on the plants, but a small amount of ash did fall there.

The second and larger eruption occurred on Mt. Redoubt in late April of 1990. Mt. Redoubt is located across Cook Inlet and is nearly straight across from the plants. It was about sixty miles away.

This was one of the most awe-inspiring things I have ever witnessed. The weather was clear, and the view from the plant was perfect. It looked like an atomic bomb had been detonated over the mountain. The clouds of ash and fire looked like a huge mushroom cloud hanging above the mountain.

We had to organize people from maintenance and the operations departments to protect the plants from the ash fallout that was coming. All of the large turbines and combustion engine filters were going to have to be changed frequently. These folks worked around the clock for over two weeks trying to keep this equipment running they were successful and the plants kept running smoothly. Mt. Redoubt still stirs from time to time, and sometimes smoke can be observed above the mountain coming from the crater

These plants have been improved over the years, and the production rates continued to go up. Someone told me that the new plants had paid for their construction in the first two years of operation. We were making around three thousand tons of ammonia every twenty-four hours. The urea plants were doing the same: about three thousand tons a day. All of our plants were running at their maximum rates most of the time, and it paid off.

These plants have had an extraordinary safety record over the thirty years that I worked there. I feel privileged to have had the opportunity to work for Unocal. The wages were good, and the benefits they offered have been excellent. I retired in late 1999.

Shortly after I retired Unocal sold the plants to a Canadian-based company. They are still in operation today. Unocal sold out to Chevron Oil Company a few years later. I was sad to hear about it because Unocal was one of the last wholly-owned American oil companies.

Part Two
Adventure in Alaska

The stories told in this book happened all over the state of Alaska, and they are true. The areas where they occurred will be explained in detail so that you will feel like you are with me in a walk across Alaska. I have included pictures so that you will be able to see the things I have seen. It is my sincerest hope that you will have the same sense of awe and inspiration that I have had about Alaska. I have been truly blessed to have had the opportunity to hunt, fish, and explore in Alaska. The stories told here are of trips that I remember as being more exciting and dangerous than others. We have been in all of the areas described in this book many, many times where nothing went wrong.

My first experience with fishing in Alaska was on the Kenai River at a place known as Poacher's Cove. My two daughters and I had come to this spot to see if the fishing was as good as we had heard it was. The first thing I saw was that there were fish jumping all across the river. You couldn't look away and then back at this river without seeing the fish finning and jumping. The water color was a grey turquoise, so we could not see the fish down in the water. I had rigged two poles with treble hooks for my daughters and one for me with a shiny lure. On my fifth cast something took the lure, and the fight was on. The fish turned out to be a bright king salmon that weighed in at fifty-five pounds. I could not believe that I had landed this fish because I was using fifteen-pound line. We spent the rest of the day enjoying the fishing. My daughters were having the time of their lives. They were casting the baited treble hooks and were catching a fish on every other cast. Most of these fish were snagged in the back. We kept the king and several red salmon; all of the others were released back into the river. When talking to one of my friends he had told me that if I was going to use bait that I should hide behind a tree when baiting my hook. After this trip I started to think he might be right. It was hard for me to believe that fishing could be this good anywhere but it was.

As I have mentioned earlier, my father-in-law was the pastor of the Soldotna Church of God. This is where we went to church and met most of our friends. One Sunday afternoon after church my wife and I were setting at our kitchen table when someone knocked on our door. I didn't know it at the time but this man was to become my best friend. His name is Don McGhee. He was twenty-six, and we were to share most of these adventures together. Don has lived in Alaska for over fifty years.

He came in and sat down at the table without saying a word. After a while he said, "Would you like to go fishing?" to which I said sure. When he got up to leave he said, "I'll pick you up in the morning." This was the shortest conversation I've ever had with anyone.

The next morning Don and I drove to Binges Landing, just past Sterling, Alaska. The road to the boat launch was dirt with a little gravel on it and was barley passable. When we got to the boat launch I noticed that there was very little room to maneuver the boat so we could launch. Don finally managed to get the boat into the water and proceeded to park the truck and trailer. Great care must be taken getting out on the Kenai River from here because of the rapids just below the launch.

Don headed the boat up river to the confluence of the Kenai and Little Keeley Rivers. He put the boat on the bank just upstream of the Little Keeley, and we tied the boat to some trees. There is an old cabin here that has been here for as long as anyone can remember. It is situated on a fairly level area about seventy-five yards from the river at the top of a high, sloping bank. The cabin is a one-room log building about fifteen feet square with a sod roof. Inside there are two bunks and a small built-in table. There is a wood-burning stove to provide heat and to cook on. The door of this cabin faces up river, and it has two small four-pane windows, one on each side. The windows are about twenty-four inches square. As far as I know the cabin is still there today.

Don and I used the cabin frequently when we were fishing and hunting in this area. Some of our most memorable trips were here. It's rumored that this cabin was used as a stopover for the dogsled teams that were used to deliver mail to the Kenai Peninsula communities in earlier times. I don't think anyone knows for sure who built this cabin. On this trip we caught rainbow and Dolly Varden trout. It was a beautiful day, and the trip went well.

As Don and I became more acquainted we discovered that we were alike in many ways. He is also an outdoors man and loves hunting fishing and exploring.

There are always some trips that will have humor and fear at the same time, this trip had both.

Don and I, along with my brother-in-law Gene Bybee, were fishing on the Kenai River at the cabin on the Little Keeley. The Kenai River is about one hundred yards wide at this spot. There are several long narrow islands on the other side of the river.

Around noon we saw a small black bear on the far side of the river. He was just wandering around on the bank looking for something to eat. Gene decided he was going to go over and shoot it. Don and I asked him why he wanted this bear. It was a small bear and looked to be around two years old. All he said was that he wanted it.

We were using my boat on this trip; it was an eighteen-foot Hews Craft. It had four seats, and the center part of the windshield could be opened, allowing us to exit the boat across the bow. As soon as Gene got in the boat and started the motor the bear ran back into the brush and trees.

But Gene was determined and went across the river anyway. When he made it across he beached the boat and went into the woods after the bear. Not long after Gene had gone after the bear it reappeared and crawled into the boat. I suppose it had smelled the fish odor in the boat and was checking it out.

When Gene returned to the boat the bear was still in it Don and I started jumping up and down and hollering trying to tell him about the bear. Apparently Gene couldn't hear us because he shrugged and climbed up on the bow of the boat. When the bear felt the boat move it exploded into action. It ran through the open window and knocked Gene backwards off of the bow. All of this took place in a matter of seconds. When Gene got up and we realized he wasn't hurt, Don and I laughed until our sides hurt. Gene didn't get the bear.

The look on his face was worth a lot, and it's one of those things you never forget.

Gene ByBee with the boat just before going after the bear

Sometimes things happen during our life's journey that defy explanation. Don and I still talk about one of those trips. We didn't understand what it was that was happening, and I suppose we never will. The things that happened here are true and happened, just the way I have written them down.

We were at the cabin on the Little Keeley River on a combination fishing and hunting trip. We had planning on being here for at least a week or until we bagged a moose. On the first day of the hunt we didn't see anything worth taking, so we returned to the cabin and decided to do a little fishing before turning in.

53

It was one of those really dark nights, and we had to use a flashlight to bait our hooks. It was so dark that you couldn't see your hand if it was in front of your face. I think we both noticed the light at about the same time. It was not natural and was very small, and brighter than any star we had ever seen. The stars weren't visible because it was a cloudy night.

We had no idea of how far away it was, but it suddenly grew much larger and was so bright that we had to cover our eyes. After it had passed over I took my hands away from my eyes and couldn't believe what I was seeing. Every thing in my field of vision was lit up in a strange sort of light. The first thing I noticed was that there were no shadows, and the light seemed to be following its source. The mountains in the distance went dark, then the trees, and then the river where we were standing. It felt like everything was happening in slow motion. From the time we first saw this light until it passed over us couldn't have been more than a few seconds.

Don grabbed the flashlight and headed towards the cabin. I had to tell him to slow down, because I couldn't see the trail and was having a hard time keeping up with him.

Once we were inside of the cabin we crawled into our sleeping bags. You can imagine how dark it was inside of the cabin after we turned the flashlight off.

We were discussing what we saw, things like, was it the landing lights on a plane, swamp gas, or perhaps a ball of lightning? Everything we could think of didn't fit, mainly because there was absolutely no sound when it went over, and it was moving at an incredible speed. It was moving faster than anything either of us had ever seen before. I was talking when Don told me to be quiet. He said, "It's coming back."

I'll never know how he knew it was coming back but it did. When the light was over the cabin again it stopped and remained over the cabin. The inside of the cabin was full of the same strange light, but it wasn't as bright. Once again I noticed that there weren't any shadows. I could see the smallest details, like the writing on a can of coffee, nails, and spider webs, and it all stood out in perfect clarity, without shadows. Don and I didn't remember anything after that. The next thing either of us recall is waking up the next morning.

On the trip down river Don told me that if I ever mentioned this to anyone he would deny that it had ever happened. I know Don better than that, and if anyone asked him about this trip today, he would tell the truth just as I have done.

Sometimes a hunting trip will turn into a wonderful opportunity to see into the past. You can never be sure of what you'll run into, and some of it can be truly amazing. It makes you wonder about the people who were here in this place before you came along. On this trip we had one of those opportunities.

Don and I spent a great deal of time hunting and exploring on Tustumena Lake. It is one of Alaska's largest lakes, being twenty-three miles long and five-miles wide. A long, wide valley between the mountains at the upper end of the lake terminates at Tustumena Glacier. There are many small streams dumping into the lake, including those coming from the glacier. The water color is a grey turquoise but clears up when you are closer to shore. The Kasilof River is the outlet of the lake and terminates in Cook Inlet.

Sometimes getting onto the lake can be a problem. There is a channel usually on the far right of the outlet, but early and late in the year the water is shallow. Don and I got out of the boat and pushed it up river until we had sufficient water to use the motor. As we started up the lake it began to rain, and the farther we went the harder it rained.

We pulled in at an old, two-story structure made of logs about halfway up the lake on the left bank. Don told me that people called it "Tustumena Lodge." It was situated on a bluff about twenty feet above the lake and had one large window and a door facing the lake. There was a smaller, single-story log building sitting next to it, about thirty feet away in the trees. I had seen two or three smaller sheds located behind the larger structures. After securing the boat we took all of our gear and went inside of the largest building. The rain continued to fall, and if anything, it was increasing in volume.

Don and I walked through the building and looked at the homemade furniture. It was apparent that no one had lived here for a very long time. There were two rooms on the upper floor, and each room contained a bunk with a thin pad on the springs. It had a wood-burning cook stove in the kitchen that appeared to be very old. It was in remarkable condition. The table and chairs were homemade out of planks and small logs. In the front room it was the same: none of the furniture had been bought at a store.

On the front room wall there was an old shipping crate nailed to the wall. It contained books and magazines. When I looked at some of the magazines they were dated as far back as 1920. I picked up a book. It was an original copy of *Call of the Wild*. Inside of the cover it was signed, "To Hattie from Jack London." The pages of this book had turned a rich golden brown from age and were a little brittle; otherwise it was in excellent condition. Upstairs we found a pair of high, button shoes made for a small child; there was another larger pair, probably made to fit a woman.

When we looked around outside we discovered an old Fairbanks Morse generator in one of the small sheds. It was a single-piston, gas-driven machine with a four-foot wheel attached to it. On the wheel a large weight had been mounted to the spokes on one side.

From what I could figure out, when the single piston fired it would move the weight to the top. Then the weight would fall to the bottom and bring the piston into firing position again. I don't know how old it was because the markings were unreadable. I'm sure it would only produce enough electricity to power a few light bulbs. There was also an outhouse and what looked like a horse shed inside of a triple-pole corral.

Don and I spent four days here, and I read the Jack London book during this time.

We never took anything from any of the places we visited. All of these things had belonged to someone in the distant past, and we both agreed that it should stay just as we had found it. I have often wondered what happened to the people who lived here so long ago. Don and I decided to leave on the forth day because it was still raining and looked like it wasn't going to stop anytime soon.

Tustumena Lodge

Alaska used to have two moose seasons: one was in August, followed by another one in November. Don's brother-in-law Mark and I went on a hunt in November that resulted in our having to be rescued. On this hunt there was a light snow cover, and it was twenty-five degrees below zero. This trip emphasizes the importance of letting someone know where you are going.

We wanted to hunt an area known as the Mystery Creek Drainage. This area runs along a buried pipe line that had been built to Anchorage from the Kenai gas fields. To get there we would have to drive south of Soldotna to the base of the Kenai Mountains. Once there we would turn left on Mystery Creek Road. This was not state maintained and was more of a trail than a road.

We were in my jeep that had been modified for off-road travel; it had a hard top and two seats. The front bumper held two five-gallon cans of gasoline, and it had a tow bar so it could be towed. The only problem with this vehicle was that it had a Buick V-6 engine in it. It turned out that the engine was too powerful for the drive-line components.

After we loaded the equipment we thought we would need for this trip we drove to Mystery Creek Trail, about forty miles away. Mystery Creek Trail terminated at the gas line, which was about twenty miles from the highway. The trail that ran along the pipe line was very rough. It crossed several streams and generally ran along the side of the mountains. There were three emergency air strips for small planes located at several places along this trail.

At the third airstrip Mark and I noticed a trail heading down to Cook Inlet. It was wide enough for the jeep, and we headed down it to see where it went. It terminated a few hundred yards from Cook Inlet. There was a cabin here made out of planks, and an old Model-T Ford. No one was around, and it appeared to have been abandoned. When we looked around we found an old grave site not far from the cabin. The inscription on the marker was not readable; it had been there for a very long time.

We decided to drive around here and look for moose. We hadn't gone far when the front wheels of the jeep fell into a hole beneath the muskeg. (*Muskeg is a form of moss that grows on the ground in Alaska. It can be 18 to 20 inches thick.*) When I tried to get out of this situation we heard one of the front axles break and were forced to use jacks and boards to get out of the hole.

With the axle broken Mark and I knew that we would not be able to return to the highway, some sixty miles from where we were at. We knew that we were in trouble, but we also knew someone would be looking for us because we were supposed to be back early in the afternoon.

We built a good fire and started preparing the cabin for the night. An airplane flew over us and made several passes. We learned later that it was Mark's dad, Matt. Later that night we heard a vehicle coming down the trail. When it got there we saw that it was Don and another one of our friends. We all decided to spend the night and try to get the jeep out in the morning.

The next morning Don hooked a chain to his bumper and took the jeep under tow. His truck didn't have the right sized ball on the tow bar. We didn't get far. On the first steep hill the tow bar on the front of the jeep fell down and hit the frozen trail. When that happened, it jerked the bumper off of Don's truck, and it flew completely over the top of the jeep. After a little discussion it was decided that we would return to town and get another truck to try it again. Don and I borrowed a heavy-duty Ford 4x4 from one of our friends who owned a service station in Soldotna; this time we were successful.

Matt told us we should get out and walk over the hills when we were hunting. He said they had seen at least fifty large bulls on both sides of the trail within fifty yards of it. I don't know if he was joking or not, but I had no reason to disbelieve him either.

The jeep Mark and I were using when the axle broke

Sometimes when you think you have all of the bases covered and have thought of every conceivable situation that could happen, you haven't. This trip is an example of some of the things that can go wrong on one of these trips into the bush and how dangerous they can be.

Don's brother-in-law Mark Humecky and I decided to go out and look for grizzly bear. We were going to go in my four-wheel-drive pickup and thought we were prepared for whatever we might get into. We drove south of Soldotna to a village known as Ninilchik, which is about a forty-five minute drive from Soldotna. I had decided to take my daughters with us because it was a beautiful day and they were hollering to go. My oldest daughter, Jenice, was six years old, and my youngest daughter, Joretta, was four.

Just before we got to Ninilchik we turned left on a gravel road. This road was maintained by the state for about three miles where it ended at a school-bus turnaround. From here the road turned into a narrow dirt trail that was not maintained. The trail traversed over hills and through low-lying areas where small creeks sometimes crossed it. We began to notice that the spring runoff from melting snow and rain had eroded the trail in some places so that we had to leave the trail to continue on. In one of these washed-out places we got stuck at the bottom after crossing a small stream. Mark and I, using a shovel and a handyman jack, started working to get the pickup out of the mud.

This area is heavily forested with spruce, birch, and other varieties of trees. It was also covered with a lot of brush, such as willow and alder. My daughters were getting restless, so I let them out of the pickup and told them to stay on the trail close to us. Mark and I were still working to get the pickup out of the mud. It started to rain a little, but it turned out to be a heavy shower that passed over quickly.

Finally we managed to get the truck out of the mud. My girls starting yelling and making a general fuss, so I admonished them and told them to be quiet. But they persisted and wanted me to come and see what they had found. When I got to where they were the hair on the back of my neck stood up.

There were large, plate-sized bear tracks crossing the trail, and I could see rain spatter marks on the trail, but none in the tracks. That bear had crossed the road after the heavy rain shower, and my kids were on the road when he had crossed. I never took my children hunting with me again until they were old enough to understand the dangers.

Flying in Alaska can be exciting, and in some instances dangerous. The weather can be a factor, as well as mechanical problems while in flight. On this trip the weather stranded us for three weeks, and there was a mechanical problem that forced us to take another plane to the island where we were going to hunt deer.

Some of Alaska's Islands have Sitka black-tail deer on them, and we have hunted on many of them. This trip was going to be on

Montague Island, situated about sixty miles south and east of Seward Alaska towards Prince William Sound.

Don and I left Soldotna and drove to the small airport in Seward. The drive from Soldotna to Seward is about one hundred miles. The sky was clear, and we were looking forward to the trip. I think it was around ten A.M. when we arrived at the airport where we contacted the charter that was going to fly us to the island.

After we had the aircraft loaded with our gear it took off heading out over Resurrection Bay. The plane was a large Beaver Aircraft that had plenty of room for us and our gear. It was a wheeled plane and would land on the beach at San Juan bay on Montague Island.

Shortly after takeoff the engine backfired and started to sputter. The pilot cursed a few times and said something about this problem was supposed to have been fixed. I could see the propeller stop and then start to turn again. It was a very tense moment. When the plane started to fall off and was headed towards the water the pilot straightened it out and headed towards the landing strip. The engine was still sputtering and cutting out occasionally; it was obvious that it wouldn't fly for much longer.

The airstrip was about two miles in front of us, and the plane was dropping faster than the pilot wanted it to. We hit the runway pretty hard and bounced several times before coming to a stop, after which the engine quit and couldn't be restarted. We found out later that a couple of the pistons had seized up.

After we had gotten off of this plane the charter company brought out another one. It was a Cherokee and was much smaller than the Beaver. It had a tricycle landing gear that I didn't care for at all. I felt that landing on the beach was safe, but the wheels on this plane weren't made for landing on the sand.

They told us that we would have to leave some of our gear behind because the Cherokee couldn't haul as much as the Beaver could. We were told that they had a tent and some gear at San Juan point so we could leave our tent and cots. Once this plane was loaded we took off again, and this time we didn't have any problems.

My concerns about landing on the beach were unfounded, but it still made me nervous. After we had unloaded the plane on the beach the pilot told us the tent was in the tree line about three hundred yards from where we were. When we finally got to where the tent was we were shocked at what we saw. The tent was an old, double-walled, army-issue tent, and it had collapsed from last year's snow. Don and I spent the rest of the day getting this tent set up and a good camping area prepared.

The trees are very large on this side of Montague Island. It is a rain forest with many different kinds of trees and brush. A lot of them have fallen down, and climbing up the mountain was difficult at best. Most of the downed trees are so big that you have to walk around them to continue on up the mountain. Don and I went up, and we both got fine bucks on the first day of the hunt.

On the second day we explored along the beach and found many interesting things washed up on the shore. There were glass floats used on Japanese fishing boats to hold up their nets all along the beach. We also found a large aluminum fishing boat that had been grounded by a storm. It was half full of sand, and the bottom had been split open in several places. Higher up on the beach a shelter had been built, probably by the men who had been on the boat. This boat had been here for a very long time, and it was geared up to commercially fish for halibut.

On the morning of the third day it was snowing, so we decided to stay close to camp. It was getting colder by the hour. When Don and I went into the tent we discovered that it had several leaks. We moved our cots around and were able to position them so that the leaks weren't hitting us, and we would not get wet while we were sleeping. The snow continued for ten days and was getting worse. The snowflakes were about the size of quarters. To continue hunting in these conditions would have been dangerous and foolhardy, so we remained in camp. Both of us knew that we would not be picked up on schedule; the weather was to bad for them to fly. I thought they might come out in a boat, since the water was calm, but they didn't.

On the eleventh day the snow had let up some and had been replaced with a heavy fog on the water. We heard a plane go over, and eventually it landed on the beach. The pilot ran up to our camp and told us to hurry. He said the weather was closing in fast. Once on the plane he took off heading in the opposite direction of Seward. I asked him where we were heading and he told me we were going to McLeod Bay. He was flying about fifty feet off of the water, following the beach. After about thirty minutes he landed on a beach and told us that another plane would pick us up. We unloaded, and he took off into the fog I have always thought that this was a foolish thing for him to have done. The visibility was really bad.

Later that same afternoon we heard another plane somewhere over the water, but we couldn't see it. All of a sudden it taxied out of the fog and snow and up onto the beach. It was a large Beaver Aircraft on floats, so it could land on the water. There were two other guys at McLeod Bay when we got there, and we all loaded our gear and deer meat on the plane. I got the seat next to the pilot, and we took off for Seward. After flying for about forty minutes the pilot said he didn't think we would be able to get into Seward, so he turned the plane and started for Whittier, Alaska. On the way a light and horn sounded on the plane's instrument panel. The pilot explained that one of his fuel tanks was out of fuel, and he switched tanks. I think there were three amber fuel lights on the plane's instrument panel. It made me nervous to be flying around in this mountain terrain in the fog and snow. The visibility was awful: we couldn't see anything until we were close to it. About this time another alarm went off. The pilot switched to another fuel tank and announced that we couldn't get into Whittier either. He turned the plane around and started to Cordova, Alaska. At one point two mountain peaks appeared in front of the plane, so he tilted the plane and flew between them. All of this was a heart-pounding experience, and I began to wonder if we were going to make it. The pilot told me we would be okay because if he had to he would set down on the ocean, and we would wait it out. As he was landing the plane the third and final tank ran out of fuel, and we coasted to a stop in the Cordova small-boat harbor. The pilot told me he had been flying around Prince William Sound for over twenty years. It would have made me feel somewhat better if he had told me this earlier.

Don and I spent Halloween night in a motel at Cordova, Alaska. I couldn't have been happier. After a shower and a good meal we went to bed and slept soundly. The next morning the storm had let up, and we were flown back to Seward, and this adventure was over.

Bears are all over Alaska, and sometimes on a hunting trip you will have to deal with them. On this trip we were hunting deer and became the hunted before it was all over. It's a strange feeling to know that the tables have been turned on you, and you are no longer in complete control.

We've made many trips to Raspberry Island to hunt deer. We've traveled by air and by boat to get there. This is the only trip that we encountered trouble with bears on Raspberry. Most of the time they won't bother you. I have seen them at a distance, but they usually stayed away from us.

For this particular trip we traveled to Raspberry Island in the Kodiak Island chain. To get there we would have to travel to Homer, Alaska, and board the Tustumena Ferry going to Kodiak. My truck was loaded down with supplies, and we loaded the zodiac rubber boat on top of the gear and tied it down. We also loaded the 15 hp engine and gas cans for the zodiac. My larger boat, a 26-foot glass ply, was already in Kodiak parked at my son's home. My son is a state trooper. He was stationed in Kodiak at the time.

Homer, Alaska, is 75 miles from Soldotna. It's about a two-hour trip. When we arrived at the terminal the ferry crew directed us to where they wanted the truck loaded. Once our equipment was aboard we went to our cabins and turned in for the night. It usually takes about 12 hours to get to Kodiak depending on the weather. Sometimes this can be a very rough trip. This one wasn't too bad.

We unloaded at the Kodiak terminal and met up with the other men who were going on this hunt. My son Tom and his friend Sven would be on the trip along with my son in-law Dennis and his two sons, William and Steven. With Don and me there was a total of seven people on the hunt.

There's a road that crosses Kodiak Island from the town. I think it's called Antone Larson Road. On the opposite side of the island on this road there's a boat launch where we launched the boat and loaded all of our gear for the trip to Raspberry. We would have to cross the bay to get to the island where we would be hunting. Once across the bay we would enter Whale Pass.

We turned to the right and started up Whale Pass. We had been traveling along at 30 mph, but the strong current here slowed the boat to 15 mph with the motors at the same rpm. Care should be taken whenever you are navigating in these waters they can be treacherous. We found the narrow straight between Raspberry and Afognak Islands, where we turned left into the narrows and out of the current. The narrows at the widest point is about three-quarters of a mile wide and at the narrowest point about three-hundred yards wide. The current here was not as bad as it was in Whale Pass. Raspberry has mountains on it, and they start going up about 200 yards from the beach. There are trees and brush scattered across the mountains with large areas of grass between them. It's a wonderful area for the animals that populate these islands. There are deer, elk, fox, and bears on this island. These are very rugged Islands. Some of the mountains go straight up from the water. Where you can climb them there are high brush alders and devil club. Devil club is a plant with thorns on it, and you will need gloves to get through them.

About halfway down the narrows we picked out a good camp site and anchored the glass ply on the Raspberry side, about two hundred feet offshore. After unloading the gear (*using the Zodiac*) we started setting up the camp. We built a covered area about 30 feet long and 20 feet wide, using poles and covering them with a tarp to keep out the rain. We set up two eight-man tents in a row, back and off to the side of the covered area. There was plenty of firewood, and we cut enough to last for a few days. This took most of the day, and we decided to start hunting deer the next morning.

It was raining when we got up the next morning, but everyone took to the field hunting anyway. I didn't see anything the first day, so Don and I came back to camp without deer. I'm not sure but I think there were two deer taken on the first day of hunting. The deer meat was hung on a pole nailed high up on two trees away from the camp and covered with a tarp to keep it dry.

Sitting around camp that night we were cooking strips of deer meat over a cottonwood fire when something moved about 100 feet from us, just inside of the trees. When we put a light on it all we could see were eyes glowing red and yellow in the light. Sven, who was a fish-and-game officer, said it was probably a brown bear and her cubs. After a while they must have gone away because we couldn't see the eyes shining in the light anymore.

These are good times when you're out in the wild. There's nothing like setting around a good fire with your family and friends. We turned in around midnight. Dennis and his two sons were in one tent. Don, Tom, Sven, and I were in the other one. It wasn't long after we turned in that we heard the tarp on the meat rattling like it was in a high wind, but there was no wind blowing at the time. Sven shot a tree by the bear, and she ran off into the woods. When morning came we went out for a look around and discovered that the bear had shredded the tarp that was protecting the deer meat but didn't get the meat. Sven and tom loaded the meat in the zodiac and took it out to the glass ply. They cleaned the zodiac and the area where the meat had been hanging with bleach and soap. After this had been accomplished we went hunting again.

The next morning prior to going up the hill to hunt we saw bear tracks on the beach and found that the zodiac had been damaged. That day I stayed in camp and repaired the small holes in the zodiac. The zodiac has two air chambers, one on each side. The right side was flat but not beyond repair.

Tom told me that day that the bear was stalking him and Sven, but they had elected not to shoot her. He said they took up a position on a hill and turned the tables on her. Once the sow knew they were on to her she left the area. On their way back to camp that evening Sven shot a deer, and they field dressed it and returned to camp. They took the meat out to the larger boat using the zodiac, and once again cleaned it with bleach and soap. That night we brought the zodiac into the camp. The next morning the zodiac was shredded on the same side, and there were large tracks all around our camp and the tents. This is the point where we started discussing the need to kill the bear or just go home. Our decision was to stay and see if the problem would go away.

The damage done to the Zodiak on the second attack by the bear

We decided to hunt in groups for safety reasons, because this bear was acting aggressively towards us. This aggressiveness is not the normal behavior for bears. All of us noticed the absence of berries on the island, and the deer were constantly on the move. It had been a hard year for the bears, and they were apparently hungrier than they usually are.

The next day Tom, Sven, and my grandson Steven went up the hill together. On the way down they went into some high alder bushes. They heard a bear cub bawling and jumping through the alders running away from them. Tom told Sven and Steven to get out of the alders and be looking for the sow to charge. When they stepped out onto the open trail they saw the sow coming from the south, in a full-out charge towards them. Sven dropped to his knee and brought his rifle up. Tom took aim from a standing position. The sow was running full out and was moving from tree to tree. Tom and Sven's rifles were moving from right to left rapidly as they looked for an opening to shoot. The bear was using cover and concealment to advance on them. They did not have an open shot at it. Tom backed up to the bluff, but it was too far to jump; it was a 30-foot drop. He noticed a large tree sticking out of the hill (like a diving board). It was about 15 feet down. Tom shoved Steven over, told Sven, and then he jumped over. Sven jumped over just before the sow got to them. They still hadn't been able to get a decent shot at her. They took up shooting positions on the beach but the sow stayed just out of view, and they didn't have the opportunity for a good shot. The sow followed them all the way back to camp as they walked along the rocky and uneven beach.

Once everyone was back in camp that evening we discussed the issues and decided that we would shoot this bear if she visited the camp again. She had charged some of our party and was exhibiting an aggressive nature that was dangerous to all of us. We built up a large fire and turned in for the night.

Shortly after we turned in that night something ran into our tent and knocked Sven completely out of his cot. Sven started hollering, "Bear, bear!" and began shooting at it. Everyone in our tent was sitting up with a pistol in his hand. It was scary to realize that this bear had actually been in the camp again.

The next morning we decided to break camp and head home. We decided as a group that the hunting was very slow (four deer out of seven hunters in six days), and the risk with this bear was too high. As we were leaving we noticed there was another party of hunters that had came in and set up camp in an old cabin about a mile from where we'd camped.

We had been home for about a week when an article came out in the papers about a bear mauling in the same area where we had been hunting. Apparently a hunter was cleaning his deer when the bear attacked him. He didn't get to his rifle, so he defended himself with his hunting knife. This man was in his 60s, and he actually killed the bear with his knife and crawled off of the mountain to the beach. I have never heard of anyone killing a bear with a knife and surviving the attack before, but he did. All of us agreed that this was probably the same bear that had given us so much trouble.

Injury is one of the worst things that can happen on a trip into the Alaskan bush country. On this trip one of our hunting partners sustained a very serious wound that required many stitches.

This trip was on the mystery creek trail where it meets the pipeline. There is a seismograph trail that leaves mystery creek trail at a forty-five degree angle heading up into the mountains. The seismograph trail is about twenty feet wide and twists and turns for about six miles, where it terminates in a stand of trees at the top of the mountain. We had decided to use our three horses as pack animals on this trip because we were walking in for about fifteen miles.

On the way in we noticed a large black bear was following us, so I told Monte and Charles to keep going, and I would deal with the bear. We had just passed a bend in the trail, and I was going to wait for the bear here. I waited for about 30 minutes and thought that the bear should be close enough for me to scare him off. When I peeked around the bend the bear was nowhere to be seen, he had apparently known I was there and had left the trail.

After I caught up with Monty and Charles we saw the bear following us again. I tried to ambush him again with the same results, so we gave up and continued on our way. There were several other bears on this trail, and I began to worry that they might become a problem. We made the tree line and kept going for about two miles to get away from the bears.

When we made camp the horses started acting up, and we had to keep guard on them through the night. Several bears visited our camp that night. The next morning we decided to leave the area because of the large number of bears that were here. When we got back to the seismograph trail, just as we stepped out of the trees, there was a large brown bear standing on its hind legs in the middle of the trail. Monty and I lifted our rifles and took aim; we didn't want to kill this bear, so Monty and I decided not to fire unless her ears went flat against her head.

Her ears went flat, and our shots went off at the same time. The bear fell forward on her face, and she was probably dead before she hit the ground. Monty and I knew that the season was closed for brown bear hunting, but we didn't have a choice this time. She was going to attack us. All three horses went wild and broke loose, running down the trail. Nearly all of the gear they were carrying started flying off of the pack frames. It was scattered all over that trail. We knew that the people who were joining us on this hunt would be coming up the trail today, so we didn't go after the horses. Monty and I started skinning the bear because Fish and Game would require the hide. This bear had a beautiful hide. She was a rich brown except for a blond V running down her back.

In the process of skinning Monty was holding his knife in his right hand. It was pointing away from him while he worked on one of the bears paws. Every time he hit a place that was tough his knife would flash up and was coming too close to me. I told him to switch hands or do something different before he got me with his knife. He reversed the knife in his hand so that the point was now pointing towards him. He had the paw in his left hand and was pulling the knife through some tough gristle when it suddenly cut through and went into his leg up to the hilt. His knife had a six-inch blade and was one and a half inches wide. Monty had just sustained a very serious wound to his leg, and we were six miles from our vehicles and sixty miles from a doctor. He was very lucky the blade didn't hit an artery and had missed the bone. It was bleeding profusely. Monty asked Charles to look in a pack that was on the trail for his sewing kit. It was there, and Monty threaded a large, straight needle with white thread. Then he began sewing up the two-inch gash on his upper thigh; the stitches were at least one inch wide, and I still don't know how he was able to do it. Once he had six or seven stitches in the wound it almost stopped bleeding. The others showed up about this time, and they had the horses and gear with them. We had to carry the hide down the mountain because the horses wouldn't even get close to it.

Monte just before his accident

Monty's leg wound healed up just fine once the doctor cleaned it and put in the proper stitches. This was to be the only serious injury we ever suffered on one of our many trips into Alaska's bush country. I never went hunting again without having suture needles and pliers in my pack.

Fish and game flew a helicopter up to the bear carcass and said the shooting of the bear was justified. They auctioned the hide off and told us that it went for a good price. The money was given to charity.

Sometimes things happen so fast that you don't have time to react. On this occasion I was ice fishing on Scout Lake in Sterling Alaska. This lake is on part of Ray and Gloria McNutt's homestead. My wife and I visited them often. They were some of our best friends.

It was a beautiful winter day, and I decided to go ice fishing on Scout Lake in Sterling. The temperature was twenty below zero, so I knew the ice would be safe and would hold the weight of me and my snow machine. After unloading the snow machine I drove it a little ways out onto the lake and drilled a hole in the ice. The fishing was good. I caught and landed several nice 12-inch trout. When I was done fishing I went up to Ray and Gloria's house to have some coffee and pick up my wife.

The next day we went to the lake again. (I really enjoyed ice fishing.) After my wife went in to visit Gloria I went down to the fishing hole I had drilled the day before. When I stepped off of the snow machine I broke completely through the ice. Somehow I managed to grab the running board of the snow machine before going completely under the ice. Every time I tried to pull myself out of the water the machine would tilt towards where I had broken through the ice. I was losing strength very fast and knew that I didn't have much time left to get out of the water. That's when I realized I had left the machine running. Usually I would have turned it off, but for some reason this time I didn't.

I reached up to the throttle on the machine and pushed it all the way down. The machine leaned over, and I thought for a moment that it would fall into the hole and take me with it to the bottom of the lake. When the track started to spin it moved the machine in a half circle around the hole and then grabbed and pulled me out onto the solid ice. I jumped on the machine and went up to the front door of Ray's house as fast as I could. My clothing had already started to freeze, and it was getting hard to move.

When Gloria saw me she knew exactly what had happened, and she sprang into action. Between her and my wife they managed to get me into the shower. They turned the shower on using warm water and told me to undress. After a while they told me to sit down in the warm water that had filled the tub. They put my clothes in the dryer and brought me warm soup to drink. I sat in the warm water until I stopped shivering, and when my clothes were dry I got dressed. After I was dressed we called Fish and Game to come out and mark the hole so no one else would fall in it. When the Fish and Game officers were finished marking the hole they told us that Scout Lake had underwater springs in it. Apparently there were several of them, and one of them was close to where I had drilled the hole in the ice. God had his hand on me that day.

I would like to take you up north to the Little Susitna River where it crosses the old Denali Highway. For hunting in this area we used several different kinds of all-terrain vehicles. We hunted moose and caribou here. The terrain is very rough and can be difficult to traverse, as some of these stories will reveal.

To get to the Little Susitna River we will have to drive 357 miles from Soldotna to Cantwell, Alaska. At Cantwell we will turn right on the Denali highway and travel about 60 miles to where the Little Sue crosses the road. Just before getting to the bridge on the river there is a gravel pit on the right. This gravel pit is the staging area for hunters going in to hunt along the Little Sue and the mountains that run along beside it.

The trail starts at the gravel pit and generally follows the river for about 10 miles. There are large mud holes, steep hills, and one rather large river to cross before you start climbing up into the mountains. The river we have to cross is about five miles in on this trail, and the trail is very rough. Don and I and one of my brothers-in-law were on this trip. Don was on his four-wheeler, and my brother-in-law Dennis and I were in my eight-wheel-drive Argo. We made the river crossing okay because it was lower than it usually is at this time of the year.

After crossing the river the trail runs through some swampy areas before it starts up into the mountains. We made it to the high country and picked another trail that we wanted to hunt and went in for another 15 miles, where we set up our camp.

The next morning we got in our vehicles and started the hunt. The terrain here is mostly open, but there are heavy spruce forests in the valleys. Wherever there are a lot of alder bushes coming down the mountains there are spruce trees scattered out among them. This terrain is perfect for moose, bear, and caribou. Dennis and I chose a ridge going up the mountain and followed it up to the top. Once on top we discovered that there was a bunch of large alders scattered around the swales and mounds. As we moved along we came upon a place that had been carved out of the mountain by rain and snow runoff. It was steep, but we thought we would have a better view of the valley if we went down into it. Once we had gone down the steep bank we went over to the edge and looked over.

We watched the valley for two hours and didn't see anything moving, so we decided to look around this spot for a while. When we started driving we discovered we were in a large hole that had very steep sides all around it. It was about six acres in size, and we couldn't climb out of it. The banks had loose gravel on them, and the wheels on the Argo would just spin out on the gravel; there was nothing to wench to. There was only one way we could get off of this mountain now, so we pulled over and looked at it. There was a very large patch of alder bushes growing out of the side of the mountain where we had to go down. The alder extended down for at least half a mile, and there were large spruce trees scattered through it. Alder bushes usually grow out of the side of the mountain and then turn up, so it looks like they are growing straight up when viewed from the valleys. This patch of alder contained rather large branches, and the bases of them were as large as my arm.

The vehicle we were in had eight wheels that extended out from the side; there were four on each side. The axles that held these wheels on were one-and-a-half-inch steel shafts. After considering this for a while we decided that the grade wouldn't be a problem because the alder should hold us back. I started the Argo and inched it forward onto the first set of alders. When the Argo tipped forward on the steep downgrade I applied the brakes so we wouldn't get moving too fast. Applying the brakes had no effect. The branches of the alder bushes got between the wheels and the body of the Argo and lifted it off of the ground. It was like we were on greased rails. The slick bark of the alder acted as a lubricant, and we started going down faster and faster. I had absolutely no control on where we were going. I yelled at Dennis and told him to jump clear of the Argo if it looked like we were going to hit a spruce tree. Spruce trees were flashing by, and I saw the Argo pass over several large logs on the way down. We must have been moving at forty or fifty miles an hour on that ride. We came to a stop on a little bench at the bottom of the alders and just sat there for a while. Neither of us could talk. Once again God had his hand on me, and I had survived.

After this happened we had a successful hunt and returned home without any other problems.

On at least two different occasions we experienced trouble crossing the river on the Little Susitna trail. My Argo and three wheelers had a tendency to float in deeper water.

On one of these occasions Don and I arrived at the river and found that it was running higher than normal. Because of the Argo's tendency to float in water more than two feet deep I didn't want to try it. The river we were trying to cross comes around a bend and straightens out. It also widens for about two hundred yards and slows down. Just past the crossing area and a little downstream it picks up speed again, and there are rapids here caused by large rocks lying on the bottom.

Don thought he could get across and wanted to pull a line over so he could help me get across. I was still reluctant to try it, but Don persisted and won out. We were going to try it. There was a man and woman there waiting to see if we made it across.

Don went upstream a little ways and started to cross. He bounced around some, but he managed to get across. Once he was on the other side I drove upstream and attached the line to the front of my Argo. Don started pulling, and I was committed to making the crossing. The Argo started floating down the river, and I realized then that I should have started across from down the river. Slack got in the line, and I picked up speed. When the wheels on the left side of the Argo hit the large rocks it tilted up and almost went over. I was standing on the left side of the Argo and holding on for dear life to the right side. The lady who was standing on the bank watching said, "Oh, my God, where's a camcorder when you need it? That's one of the wildest thing I've ever seen!" I don't know what it looked like, but I do know that I was scared.

Eventually the Argo stopped on the far bank, facing up river. The engine compartment was full of water, but the engine was still running. Once I got on the bank and examined the Argo I found out that one of the wheels was almost broken off, and the welds on two others were cracked. When I kicked the bent wheel it fell off, so I had to go back across the river to town and have it fixed. I didn't have any problems with crossing this time, and when I returned we continued with the hunt. This was the only real problem I ever had crossing this river.

On another trip to this same area I had to rescue my brother-in-law Gene. He was riding a three-wheeler, and on our way out he started floating down the river. I think he did the right thing by turning downstream and angling across. When he did get to the other side he was standing in the water about waist deep, holding his machine in place against the current. The bank where he landed was too high for him to get out of the river. So I crossed over and pulled him and his machine out, after which I built a good fire so he could get warm and dry out. He was shivering from the cold.

If you're going to be out in this country it's a good idea to have a wench on your vehicles; that way when one of these situations happen you can be of some help to others. It's also a good idea to make sure that your vehicle is in top condition before you go. That way you know you can rely on it to bring you out again.

We were hunting moose on this trip, but I ended up with a record-class black bear instead. This bear nearly killed me after I had killed him. I had the hide tanned because the skull measured 18 inches, and the hide was an impressive six feet from nose to tail. That means he would have stood eight feet tall when standing up on his hind legs.

This hunt started at an old horse trail off of funny river road. To get there we would have to drive to Soldotna and turn right on Funny River Road just before crossing the bridge. We had my wife take us about 10 miles out on Funny River Road to where the horse trail starts. Once we were at the horse trail Don and I were planning to walk to Cold Creek Lake, a distance of nine miles.

This horse trail runs through a valley, and there are areas where it is muddy and wet for most of the year. On this day it was raining. The packs Don and I were carrying weighted about 50 pounds apiece and were mounted on aluminum frames. When we got to the lake it was almost dark, so we set up out tent and turned in for the night. The next morning I wasn't felling too good so I stayed in camp, and Don went out to look around. When he returned later that day I told him I was getting worse and maybe we should terminate the hunt and return home. He agreed with me, since I was sweating and shivering at the same time.

The next morning I felt a little better, but I had a pounding headache. So we packed up our gear and started the long walk back to the road. We hadn't gone far, perhaps two miles, when Don said, "Do you want that bear?" When I looked in the direction he was pointing I saw a larger-than-normal black bear. It was about 300 yards from where we were standing and appeared to be eating berries. I told him that this bear was very close to being the largest one I had ever seen, and I would try the shot. It was a long shot, but it hit him, and he went down. Don had fired at the same time. He said he was aiming for a heart-lung shot. I had aimed at his neck. We waited awhile before approaching the bear because he might not have been dead, and there is nothing worse than a wounded bear. Both of our shots had found there mark, and the bear was indeed dead.

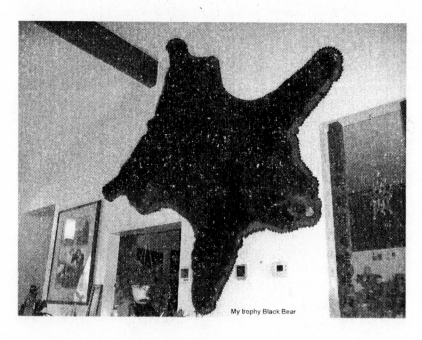
My trophy Black Bear

Now the real work would begin. Don and I skinned the bear and then cut him up into quarters, which we covered with a tarp. We had decided to return the next day to retrieve the meat. I rolled up the hide and tied it to my pack. I found out later that the total weight of the pack was 135 pounds. It was so heavy that Don had to help me get it up on my back, and I would have to carry it seven miles to the road. I couldn't take the pack off of my back because I knew that if I did I would never be able to pick it up again. When I stopped to rest I would lean up against a tree to get some relief from the weight. It seemed to me like we would never get back to the road, but finally we did, and I was able to drop the pack. I literally thought I was going to die. My shoulders and legs hurt so much that it was an hour before I could stand up again.

We returned the next day with some friends of ours to pack out the rest of the meat. Several people told me to be sure and bring out all of the fat. They said it was really good for making doughnuts. I gave the fat to the folks who wanted it and sent the rest of the meat off to have it smoked. We never wasted anything from any of the animals we killed. They were used to feed our families and the families of others who weren't able to hunt.

Ray McNutt told me how to prepare the hide for shipping. He told me to pick up some uniodized salt and rub it onto the fleshy side of the hide. I let it drain for a week and then reapplied the salt. Then I rolled it up and put it into a large game bag and delivered it to Ray. He sent it to Jonas Brothers in Denver for processing. When it came back it was beautiful. The hair was about four inches long, and it had double-felt backing sewn on the backside of the hide. This bear skin still hangs in the living room of my home.

Sheep and Goat hunting presents a completely different set of circumstances. These hunts are usually carried out on the tops of some very rugged mountains. There are rock slides to contend with, and the footing can be very dangerous indeed.

My oldest daughter Jenice had drawn a permit for mountain goat. The permit was for the area located within Day Harbor east of Seward, Alaska. She asked me if I would take her and her husband

Dennis on this hunt because I had hunted sheep and goat before. I explained that hunting goats was not easy, and we would probably have to climb up at least 5000 feet to find them.

There are goats lower down on the mountains, but they are usually looking down the mountain and will disappear if anyone tries to approach them from below. The best way to hunt goat is to climb to the top of the mountain and work your way down or around to where they are. If you're careful and move slowly you will find them and can usually get in at least one good shot before they run. It's a good idea to look at where it will fall when you shoot it. I have heard of them falling into areas where the hunter couldn't get to them, so they were lost and wasted.

We would have to drive to the Seward small-boat harbor for this hunt. The plan was to follow my charter boat in my son-in-law's 18-foot monarch river boat, east out of Resurrection Bay over into Day Harbor. Once we were there the charter boat skipper would go on with his charter for that day. He was told to come back in the evening on a specified day so we could follow him back to the Seward small boat harbor.

We went east around the far point of day harbor to a small, unnamed bay. When we looked up at the mountains there were plenty of goats scattered around at different heights. The tide was about half-way in, and there was no wind. It was a very pretty day. I landed the boat on a steep sandy beach and buried the anchor in the sand to hold it in place. We were going to scout around for a place to climb the mountains in the morning. We started off across a wide, flat area heading towards the mountains about three-quarters of a mile away. There was a small river running down the valley, but it was easy to get across.

We began to notice that the weather conditions were changing. A stiff wind was beginning to blow, and the water was getting rougher. When we looked back at the boat it had turned sideways to the bank and was being pounded by the rising tide and surf. Dennis and I rushed back to the boat and saw that it was half full of water and in danger of sinking. We would have to do something to rescue the boat. The surf was getting worse by the minute.

We picked up the anchor and threw it into the boat. The line was slack, and it was not doing any good at the time. I jumped into the surf and was trying to turn the boat so that we could pull it high enough up on the beach to let some of the water out of it. This turned out to be a serious mistake. One minute I was in knee-deep water, and then in neck-deep water. Somehow a line was in the water that was attached to the boat. It had wrapped around one of my legs, and when the surf pulled the boat out it would jerk my legs out from under me. When I lost my footing I went completely under the water. This was turning out to be a very dangerous situation.

My son in-law, Dennis, saw what was happening and rushed over to me, cutting the line that was tangled around my legs. After I was freed from the line we were able to get the boat turned and began pulling it higher up on the sandy beach. The surf was actually helping us get the boat up on the beach once we had it turned in the right direction. It was full of water, and we couldn't pull it up until a wave hit it from behind. Foot by foot we managed to get it up on the beach high enough to start baling the water out of it.

After we all changed out of our wet clothing we rested for a while and then started working on the boat. By this time the tide had turned and was on the way out. This helped with the surf, and it had subsided enough that we were able to launch the boat. Dennis started the motor and ran the boat around in circles with the plug pulled to get all of the water out of it. Once this was accomplished we loaded our gear and headed back into the more protected bays in Day Harbor. We picked out a good camping spot in the first bay on the right side of Day Harbor and pulled in to set up camp.

The next morning we climbed up the mountain behind our camp. We only carried one small canteen because there are usually small streams running off of the mountains, and you don't need a lot of water. We picked the best route up and began climbing. When we came out above the tree line we saw that there were a lot of rock slides. These would have to be crossed to get to the area where could look down the other side of this mountain.

One of these rock slides was rather wide, about 200 feet, and extended all the way to the bottom of the mountain. Dennis and I started across it and told Jenice to follow and watch her footing. When Dennis and I got across the slide we looked back and saw Jenice about halfway across. She was frozen there with fear and said she couldn't move. I moved back onto the slide and tried to calm her down enough so that she could continue on. After a while she reluctantly followed me off of the slide. I didn't realize until that moment that she was afraid of heights. We ran out of water and were forced to eat the snow that was on top of the mountain. I knew that this was not a good idea because snow will tend to make you feel thirstier, but it will help in the short term.

We didn't see any goats, so I picked an easier path down the mountain through an alder patch. Whenever you see alder on a mountain you will usually find a small stream running down thru them. There was a stream here, and we all satisfied our thirst before continuing on down to our camp.

The next morning we decided to look around from the boat to see if we could spot the goats that we knew were here. We hadn't gone far when we spotted a good goat not far from where we were camped. There was a gully leading up to a point above the goat, and they should be able to get a shot at it if they didn't hurry. He appeared to be staying around some large rocks at the head of a small sloping valley just above the tree line.

When we got back to camp I gave them some advice and told them which way to go to get above this animal. They were anxious to get started, so I cautioned my daughter about not getting her eye to close to the rifle scope before making her shot. They put on their pack gear and headed up to where the goat should be. I stayed in camp for about an hour and then went fishing. Once on the water I discovered that I didn't bring any bait or lures on this trip. I took out a pair of shiny pliers and separated them by removing the bolt that held them together. After I had one side of the pliers loose I attached a hook to a four-inch leader and tied it to the bolt hole in the pliers. I attached the line from the rod and reel through the same bolt hole, and I was ready to see if it would work. After jigging this rig for a few hours and over many likely spots I felt a strike and set the hook. What I had caught was a 25-pound halibut. This just goes to show you that it isn't always the bait you use but how it's presented. This was the only time I have ever caught a fish using a pair of pliers for bait. I don't remember if I kept the fish or threw it back. After this little fishing trip I went back to the camp for a nap.

Later in the afternoon, around four P.M., I heard a shot and then several more from where Dennis and Jenice should have been. I assumed that they had been successful in their goat hunt. Several hours went by, and I didn't see them, so I began to get a little worried; it was getting dark.

Finally around nine P.M. they walked into camp. I was relieved to see them. Dennis was carrying a heavy load of goat meat, and Jenice was carrying the head and hide. There was blood running down my daughter's face from a cut and bruise above her right eye. "Forgot the scope?" I asked.

Dennis Jenice & Charley with Jenice's Goat

She told me she had been really excited when she saw the goat and forgot about it. After they had put everything away and eaten and cleaned up, we turned in for the night.

When we got up the next morning we weren't in any hurry because this was the day my boat was supposed to pick us up. He wouldn't be here until after he finished his charter for the day. The boat coming to get us was late; it was already dark when we saw lights coming into the bay. When it got a little closer we found out it wasn't my boat. Apparently my boat was having engine problems, and the skipper had come out with another man on his boat.

They told us it was really storming when they came around Cape Resurrection. After a little discussion they decided that it would be safe to return if we got underway soon. We loaded our gear into the larger boat and tied the river boat to its stern for towing. After we were all on board the skipper started out for Cape Resurrection. Once we cleared the protection of Day Harbor it really got rough. We would have to travel about six miles in 10-foot seas with a fierce wind on it. The worst part would be going around Cape Resurrection because of the shoaling that always occurs here. Shoaling is a condition where the waves from deeper water hit the shallow areas close to shore. It doesn't help any when these waves hit the cliffs and roll back into the waves coming ashore. That was a really rough trip but we made it into Seward, and everything came through it just fine.

My daughter's goat was a good one, with horns about nine inches long, and it had good solid bases. She had it mounted, and it still hangs on her living room wall. You don't hear about many ladies having a successful hunt for goats. She is very proud of having done this, and I am proud of her.

Not all hunts are successful. Sometimes you can't find an animal that Meets Fish and Game regulations. Fish and Game requires that a moose have horns with a span of 50 inches or wider. They also require that the smaller moose have forks on

87

each side or at least one spike and a fork. The moose season has been shortened to one season beginning on August 20 and ending on September 20.

Don and I used to hunt behind Eureka lodge located on the old Glenn Highway. Eureka Lodge is a small restaurant with a few rooms to rent there is also a gas station located next to the lodge. The area here is relatively flat until you get several miles into it. It's a heavily forested area with plenty of marshes and swamps. The Little Nelchena River runs through the area and crosses the highway several miles from the lodge. The trails leading into the back country are small, muddy and rough most of the time. To get to the lodge we had to travel a distance of 270 miles from Soldotna.

There used to be a large population of caribou located here, and I have seen herds with at least 200 animals in them. At some point they either moved on or they don't come this far down anymore. It's been years since I've seen more than one or two animals here. If you travel far enough on the trails behind the lodge you will come out on the Denali Highway there are still plenty of caribou just off of the Denali Highway.

We spent a lot of time snow machining on the trails behind this lodge. It's a great place to ride, and we've enjoyed all of our trips here.

Don and I spent about ten days hunting here, and we saw a lot of bulls, but none of them were legal so we returned home empty handed. On the last day of hunting season I decided to take my Argo and hunt around the Kenai gas fields. About a mile south of my home is Irish Hills Road. When I got there I made a right turn and drove about a mile to where it ends. I unloaded the Argo and went down a wet muddy trail to where it terminated at the gas fields. I didn't see anything out on the swamp in the gas field so I started cross country, skirting the gas field.

I was driving around a small patch of alder bushes, and when I came out of them, there was a creek in front of me, about 30 feet lower than I was. Something caught my eye. It was a cow moose standing behind a tree that had fallen down. The tree was lying at about a 45-degree angle with the ground. While I was watching this cow I saw a movement to my left across the creek. It was a legal bull, and he looked to be in perfect health. He was just standing there facing me with his nose about four inches above the ground. I took the shot from where I was sitting in the Argo. I was about 50 yards from the bull. He went down, and then the real work started. I cleaned and quartered him, put the meat into game bags, and then loaded it into the Argo. I tied the horns on top of the meat just behind the seat.

Moose I got On the Last Day Of The Season

When I started driving back to where I had left my truck I noticed that the Argo was straining with the load. There must have been 600 pounds of weight in the Argo, not counting my 200 pounds. There was a steep bank about 20 feet high on the trail just short of where I had parked my truck. When I started up this bank the front of the Argo lifted off of the ground, and it nearly flipped over backwards. The horns tied just behind my seat jabbed me in the back, causing me to let go of the throttle. When I released the throttle the front of the Argo dropped back on the ground, and it rolled down the incline and stopped.

I sat there for a little while feeling to see if the horns had penetrated my back and wondering how I was going to get up that steep incline. Finally I decided to back up the incline. I thought that the weight in the back of the Argo would hold it down. It worked, and I was soon at my truck preparing to load the Argo. When I drove across the ramps into the back of my truck I applied the brakes, but due to the weight in the Argo I ran into the rear window of the truck, which shattered. This moose season had been costly.

Shortly after this trip I sold the Argo and ended up with a six-wheel drive Polaris. It's built like a small pickup with a cargo area that dumps and has two bucket seats and a steering wheel. It would prove to be a much better vehicle for the type of hunting and exploring that I do.

I have only been on one guided hunting trip since coming to Alaska. This trip was provided to me by Ray McNutt. Ray was a master guide. His wife Gloria was the Sterling Alaska postmaster. Ray had taught me how to hunt and deal with most of Alaska's big game. The advice he gave me was invaluable and has saved me from harm in more than one instance. He is gone now but he will live on in people's memories for many years.

My wife and I had known Ray and Gloria McNutt for as long as we've been in Alaska. Ray and Gloria had been here for a long time. They homesteaded in Sterling, Alaska, sometime in the early fifties. When Ray was away from home attending to his guide service I would help Gloria whenever she needed something, things like repairing her washing machine or dryer. Ray told me he really appreciated my help around the place when he was gone and wanted to take me on a sheep hunt. I told him he didn't need to do that. I told him I didn't help Gloria to gain favors from him. I also told him I would do the same thing for any of our friends who were in a similar situation.

Ray got a little upset with me and said, "What? You can help me, but I can't do anything for you?" I had to relent, and he set a date and time for the hunt. It would be in August. He told me it would be okay if I wanted to bring along a couple of my friends. I thanked him and told him I would invite Don and his brother-in-law Kip to come along with me.

The area we would be hunting was in the Wrangle Mountains that run along the Alaskan and Canadian border. We would have to drive to Northway, Alaska, where Ray would pick us up in his plane. Northway is 521 miles from Soldotna, and it would take us at least 12 hours to drive there. When we arrived at Northway they were expecting us and told us to stay in the hanger until the next morning. I think Northway is an Indian village; there wasn't much there at the time.

Ray arrived early the next morning and taxied over to where we were standing. We loaded the plane, and he took off, heading to one of his base camps located somewhere in the Wrangle Mountains. The weather was overcast with heavy white clouds, and Ray flew up through them until we came out on top. From here all we could see was a few mountain peaks rising above the cloud cover. I asked him how he would be able to know where to land without being able to see through the clouds. He told me that he knew exactly where he was and mentioned that I should relax and enjoy the view. It still made me nervous to be flying around in the mountains without being able to see most of them. However I trusted Ray; he was one of the best pilots I have ever seen. He had taken Don and me up on several moose hunts in the Sterling area; all of them were successful. He had an uncanny knack for spotting game from the air and then walking to where they were the next morning.

We had been flying for a little over an hour when Ray banked the plane over sharply and started down through the cloud cover. I caught myself holding my breath, and I had a death grip on the seat I was sitting in. When we broke through the clouds there was a dirt landing strip in front of the plane, and it was running uphill from the end we were approaching. Ray made a smooth landing and taxied up to some fuel barrels, where one of his helpers was waiting with a vehicle to transport us to camp. This camp was located on Ophir Creek somewhere in the Wrangle Mountains. I was totally lost.

Ray's camp at Ophir Creek had a large, well-built log building, a corral holding many horses, and several large wall tents with wood-burning heaters in them. It was close to the creek, and we were told there was good grayling fishing here. We spent the day lounging around and fishing in the creek. These were the first grayling I had ever caught, and I was surprised to find out that their meat was almost clear and fatty. One of the camp helpers cooked them for our supper that night, and it was some of the best tasting fish I had ever eaten.

Ray's camp on Cotted Creek

The next morning they loaded four pack horses with our supplies and saddled three others for us to ride. My horse was really large, and Ray said he was gentle and trail wise. His name was Ed. We rode through some beautiful valleys to a line camp situated on the side of a mountain. Herb said we should eat dinner here before moving on because we still had a long way to go. Herb was the under guide Ray had assigned to us for this hunt. He was in his seventies and appeared to be in excellent condition for his age. We traveled along a big valley next to the white river. When we got to a crossing Herb told us to stay together and started across. There was an island in the middle of the river, and the water was about three feet deep. The island was covered with brush, and there was a large grizzly bear standing on the edge of it about forty feet from us. The bear reared up on its hind legs when we started across, but the horses didn't pay any attention to it at all.

When we were across the river the trail started up towards the high mountain valleys above the tree line. There was a lot of swamp on the side of this particular mountain, and the riding was somewhat touchy. A little later we entered a wide valley, heading up. The trail was easier than it had been for the horses. It was apparent that these horses were comfortable in the mountains. The one I was riding wouldn't go where he felt like it wasn't safe. I never tried to force him and let him pick the trail he was comfortable with.

Kip looked at me and said, "Let's race to those rocks!" and kicked his horse up to a gallop. He hadn't gone far when his horse stopped suddenly, and he was thrown over its head and landed face first in a mud bog. He wasn't hurt, so it was hard to keep from laughing at his perfect three-point landing in that mud hole. Don was leading his horse, and when I asked him why, he told me the horse needed a rest. Actually I think he was a little saddle sore. He told me later that his knees were sore and he needed a rest.

When Herb stopped he informed us that this was where we would make camp, so we set up our tents and gear. We could see there were plenty of sheep on the mountains in front of the camp. Herb hobbled the horses, and we turned in for the night, looking forward to the hunt we would start in the morning.

When it became light enough to see we ate breakfast and were preparing to move off towards the sheep we had seen the previous day. Herb told us that the larger sheep wouldn't be there; he said they would most likely be on the mountains behind the camp. So we started climbing where he led us. Herb just ran off and left us standing in his dust. I have never seen anyone go up a mountain as fast as he had just done. It took us at least two hours to get to where he was waiting for us. His comment when we caught up with him was, "I thought you guys would never get here." Apparently none of us were in as good as shape as he was. We hunted on this mountain all day and didn't see even one sheep. When we got back to camp we discovered that the horses had slipped their hobbles and were gone.

Herb told us to go ahead and hit the sack; he was going after those horses. When we got up the next morning Herb was still not back, so we went up the mountain where we had previously seen the sheep. These mountains proved to be much more rugged than the ones we had climbed earlier. Herb returned with the horses in tow later in the afternoon; you could tell he was very tired.

I think Don got his sheep first, then Kip; I didn't see one worth shooting until the last day of the hunt. It was only a three-quarter-curl ram, but I was happy with it. Don's was a full-curl ram and Kip's was a curl-and-a-quarter ram, which is a pretty good one. Herb skinned them as they were brought in and prepared the meat for transport. We were there for about five days, and then we returned to the line camp on Ophir Creek.

Ray picked us up the next day and flew us to his main camp at Nebesna. The cook at this camp was the ex-wife of one of our friends who owned a small hardware store in Soldotna. She is the only woman I have ever known that smoked cigars. She was, however, a very good cook. After lunch Ray flew us back to Northway, and we returned to Soldotna.

I understand now why a guided hunt costs so much. Ray had committed a bunch of resources to get us our sheep, and it must have cost him a lot to do it. This sheep still hangs on the wall of my home in Soldotna.

There are times when you think certain things were predestined to happen. These things will have a direct effect on you, and you realize that a greater force was involved. On this trip one of those things saved our lives.

I think this was our first attempt to hunt deer on Montague Island. Don and I, and one of our friends, Leon Smith, were going to try and get to Montague Island by boat out of Seward.

I was working a night shift and asked a friend if he would change the oil and spark plugs on my boat motor. His name was Norman Powell, and he said he would be happy to do it for me. This was on the first boat I owned in Alaska. It was a 16-foot fiberglass Skagit, and the motor was an inline six-cylinder outboard. Norman completed the work and informed me that everything was ready to go.

When I finished my night shift we started gathering up the gear needed for the hunt and drove over to Seward. Once we had the boat loaded and everything was secured we started up Resurrection Bay. We would have to go around Fox Island, located at the end of the bay. Once we rounded Fox Island we would have 40 miles of open water to cross before we reached Montague Island.

This was a foolish trip for us to undertake, and no one should attempt it in a boat as small as mine was. The boat was sound and had a "V" bottom. It was stable in the water and rode well, but it was just too small for this trip. The waters of Prince William and Blying Sound can and do get very, very rough. When you're young you think nothing will happen to you;, the bad things always happen to the other guy.

We were approaching Fox Island and noticed that the swells coming down the bay were larger than we had ever seen them before. One minute all you could see was a wall of water all around you and the land would disappear. When you were on top of a swell you could see for miles in any direction. We talked about it and decided the swells were large enough that we could plane out on them. We were making pretty good speed so we decided to go. This was our second mistake, but something intervened that stopped us from going on.

As we were rounding the island I started increasing power to the motor. When the motor was at full power we heard it backfire, and it started making a loud, continuous, popping sound. I pulled the cover off of the engine and discovered that the number three spark plug was hanging loose on its wire. Our speed had been reduced to almost nothing. I could have walked faster than we were moving. At this point I turned around and went back to a small cove located on the Resurrection Bay side of Fox Island.

We beached the boat and turned it around so that the engine was facing the beach. Apparently the number three plug had been over tightened, and the threads that held it in place had stripped out. We worked on it for several hours trying it get it fixed, but it was impossible to repair under these conditions. While we were engaged with the engine we didn't notice that the wind had picked up and was getting stronger by the moment. When we looked out of the cove, the water had three-foot breakers developing on the waves that had came up.

It was soon realized that we were going to have to stay on the island until this developing storm had passed. There was a small A-frame cabin located well above the tide line, next to the trees on the island, so we moved all of our gear into it. Then using lines and a come-along winch we started pulling the boat up on the island as far as we could. We could see that this was going to be a pretty bad storm. After we had pulled the boat as far up onto the beach as we could we secured it with several lines to the trees. The bow of the boat was facing the surf, it was a little above the high-tide mark.

Later that evening the storm had grown in its ferocity and had become one of the worse storms I've ever seen. Don and I observed rocks the size of my fist being blown along the beach like they were tennis balls. The waves going down the bay were at least twelve feet high and had six-foot breakers on top of them. Even in this cove the waves were crashing above the normal high-tide mark. The boat was taking a beating.

We went into the cabin and tried to get some sleep, but that was nearly impossible. Some of the gusts from this wind would lift one corner of the cabin, and it would drop back down again when the gusts subsided. This went on all night and into the next day. It was truly miserable.

During the evening of the second day we looked around in the trees on the island. We found one tree that we couldn't reach around with all of us holding hands. It's one of the largest spruce trees I have seen since coming to Alaska. I've never seen one larger than this one, and I've seen a lot of spruce trees. The storm started to subside on the third day that's when we found out the boat had a split on one side of the bottom. I had some fiberglass putty and hardener on the boat so we were able to repair it enough to get us back to the harbor. Later that night the wind shifted, and the next morning the water in Resurrection Bay was calm enough for us return to the harbor. When the water calmed down it was quite a job getting the boat back down the beach and into the water. When the boat was in the water we loaded our gear and started the long day's trip to the harbor. It took us eight hours to get to the harbor. It's normally a thirty-minute trip. If the number three spark plug had not failed we would have most likely perished on this trip. We didn't have full-cover suits, but we were wearing life preservers. The temperature of the water in Alaska is so cold that you can't survive much more than 45 minutes; this is true for most of the year.

Bears we have observed on the Little Susitna River trail usually didn't bother us. We've sat and watched them for hours, but on one trip a juvenile bear did come into our camp, on more than one occasion. He was after the meat that we had hung too close to the camp.

Don, my son in-law Dennis, and I went in on the Little Susitna River trail hunting for moose. We didn't have any problems with the river crossing and traveled in for about 15 miles. At one point the main trail went straight, and we noticed a little-used trail going up a valley to the right. We decided to take the smaller trail because there were no recent tracks on it. After traveling on the trail for about three miles we discovered why it hadn't been used much.

It had been raining in this area for about three weeks, and all of the trails were wet and muddy. In front of us was a large area of swamp and water that looked to be impassible. We dismounted from our machines and walked out into it for quite a ways before deciding to keep going. The swampy area went on for about a mile before we again found solid ground. We hadn't gone far before we encountered another large swamp. In all we had to cross seven different swamps on the trail before we found a suitable area to make camp. All of us were stuck at one time or another and had to be winched out. Don and Dennis were pulling trailers loaded down with camping gear, so they were having a worse time than I was. We had traveled in for another 20 miles on this trail according to our G.P.S.

It was around four P.M. when we arrived at the place where we were going to camp. All of us began unloading the gear and setting up a good camp. There was an old meat pole nailed between two dead trees. It looked solid enough to hold a moose. We were concerned that it was too close to our camp. It was about 30 feet from the tent. After discussing it we decided that since we hadn't seen any bears it would probably be okay. When we had finished cooking and eating supper we turned in for the night.

The next morning after we had eaten and cleaned up the camp we mounted our machines and continued on down the trail, hunting. There didn't seem to be many moose tracks or bear tracks, but there were caribou tracks everywhere. We had seen several large herds of caribou on the way in, and we thought that their tracks had covered the moose tracks. Don had brought along a moose call, and I asked him if I could use it. It was one of those that you blew like a whistle. The instructions said to blow short breaths once or twice and wait awhile before repeating the call. We spent most of the day in a river valley in the high mountains, glassing the slopes for moose. Later in the evening we started back towards our camp. I used the moose call sparingly and only blew on it once or twice when we were stopped. When we arrived at our camp I blew two short grunts on it, and then we cooked our evening meal. Around eight o'clock, as it was starting to get dark, I gave two short calls and put it away.

We've always kept a clean camp. All of the empty cans and trash was put into plastic bags and would be hauled out with us when we left. After picking up around camp I sat down and was watching the valley when Dennis started yelling, "Moose, moose!" When Don and I looked where he was pointing we saw two moose, and one of them was a small, "legal" bull.

They had almost walked into our camp and were about thirty yards from us. Don and I told Dennis to hurry and take the shot before it got too dark to see. Dennis took the shot, and it was a successful kill. The bull ran down into some high brush before going down. It was nine o'clock, and it was fully dark now, so we would have to clean it using lights. I brought my Polaris around and turned the lights on the moose so Dennis could see to clean him. Dennis told Don and me that he wanted to clean this one by himself because he had never done it before. It took until two o'clock in the morning for Dennis to complete the job. When the quarters were in the game bags we hung them on the meat pole and put a tarp over the pole to keep the meat dry.

It had been a really long day, and we were all very tired. After we cleaned up we turned in and went to sleep.

I don't know why I sleep light when I'm out on the trail, but I do. We hadn't been in the sack much more than an hour when I heard cans rattling between us and the meat pole. I reached up and unzipped the window flap next to my cot and looked out. I caught a fleeting glimpse of a bear in the weak firelight. He ran as soon as he heard the zipper. Dennis heard me and asked what it was. I told him we had company. but he had run off. I had barely gotten back to sleep when the meat pole fell down with a loud crash.

Dennis and I both went outside and saw a juvenile bear trying to pull the meat loose from the pole it was tied to. I fired my forty-caliber Smith and Wesson pistol in the air two or three times and yelled for him to get away. He didn't come back, so we assumed he was still running after all the commotion we made. Don had slept through all of this until I fired the pistol; then he asked us what was going on. We returned to our bunks and slept in until eight o'clock.

The next morning we decided to leave, because if we should get another moose we would have to make two trips in order to get it all out. The trip back to the staging area went well, possibly because it had stopped raining, and things were drying out. Even so I could tell that the Polaris was loaded to its maximum capacity.

Don and DENNIS on the Little Susitna Trail

Part Three
Fishing, Gold Mining,
and Snow Machining in Alaska

One of my favorite places to fish was on the upper Kenai River.
It was not as crowded as the lower river, and the fishing was
excellent. I took many friends and family members here to fish.

Bill Powell and his family came to Alaska to visit his brother
Norman. They were from Florida and had driven to Alaska in their
motor home. Norman brought them over to see us one day, and we
planned a fishing trip on the upper Kenai River. We were all going to
meet at the upper Skilak Lake campground. The plan was to spend a
few days fishing at different places along the upper Kenai. Everyone
brought their own motor homes or trailers to the campground to stay
in. There was another family from Eagle River, Alaska, who went
along on this trip they were good friends of Norman and Sue Powell.
Their names were Bill and Mary Jones. Bill was a butcher, and he
processed some of the game I got on my hunting trips. He made the
best sausage I have ever eaten.

I had brought my boat to the campground, and we decided that only
four people and I would go on each trip. We would make three trips
a day. That way everyone could fish for about four hours every day
while we were here. I knew from the first trip that we were going to
have some really good fishing.

I used light gear when I fished in the Kenai River; my rods were
five feet long, and the spinning reels were spooled with six-pound-

monofilament line. I used artificial bait on a number four hook with a small split-shot weight, about 12 to 18 inches above the lure. The artificial bait was flesh-colored and about the size of the end of my little finger. We would drift down river with the lines played out upriver. As the boat drifted along you could feel the small sinker tapping along the rocks on the bottom. They rarely got hung up on the bottom, so when your rod tip was pulled down you set the hook. I have caught a lot of trophy fish using this setup.

If the red, silver, or king salmon are in the river you will also catch them on this setup. If they aren't hitting the lure, change it to another color. Fish seem to be picky sometimes. A good bet is the Potsky fireball salmon egg with a very small gold hook buried in it.

On this trip everyone caught all the fish they wanted, and we had a wonderful time sitting around the campfire in the evenings. Mary Jones caught a good trophy rainbow and had it mounted. Bill's wife Joyce caught a trophy rainbow, and she was really happy about it. Bill Powell had his sons with him in Alaska that summer, and one of them became my son in-law, Dennis.

Tom, Bill Powell and me with our catch

Bill Powell has returned to Alaska many times over the years, and we have had a lot of fun together hunting, fishing, and exploring. I have met many of his family members, and they are good people. I feel privileged to have known them.

Norman and his family used to camp on the upper river with us a lot. We would pitch tents on the river bank and fish for several days at a time. Norman was the pastor of the Kenai Church of God. Later he was the pastor of the Eagle River Church of God.

Norman Powell, Gene, Myself and Dennis with the days catch

On another occasion my brother-in-law Roland Bowling and two of his friends, G.P. and Frank, came to Alaska to visit us. I think G.P. was one of Roland's best friends, and Frank was GP's father-in-law. I never knew what GP's real name was; everyone simply called him G.P.

I picked Roland and his friends up in Anchorage at the international airport. I needed a new engine for my boat, so we stopped by and picked it up and started home. I wasn't familiar with driving in Anchorage, and I got lost. I couldn't find my way out of town and spent a couple of hours looking for the road leading to Soldotna. Finally we got on the right road, and we made it to my home south of Soldotna. This was really embarrassing, especially since there's only one road into Anchorage and one road out.

Roland and his friends had been hearing about fishing in Alaska for a long time and wanted to try it. The next morning I took them to Soldotna to get their fishing licenses, and we went up the Kenai River for our first day of fishing. GP was an accomplished fisherman and started catching fish right away. He was having the time of his life. We spent all day fishing and returned home late in the afternoon.

The following day we took them to clam gulch to dig for razor clams. My youngest daughter Joretta was the expert clam digger in our family. She was going to show them how to do it. Clam digging is touchy and requires a special skill in order to get them without breaking their shells. I think everyone learned how to do it except for Roland; he just couldn't get the hang of it. Don came over the next day, and we planed a trip on Tustumena Lake to show them the country and do a little fishing. We would use both of our boats for this trip.

We traveled to Tustumena Road about 10 miles south of my home and followed it to where it terminates at the upper Kasilof River. After we launched our boats Roland, my son, and I got in my boat, and Don, Frank, and GP got in Don's boat. The trip upriver to the lake went okay, and there was enough water at the lake entrance, so we didn't have to get out and push the boats through the shallow entrance. When we rounded Caribou Island the lake was a little rough, so we stayed in close to the right shore and proceeded up the lake.

At one point we pulled in to shore to take a little rest before proceeding on up the lake. We visited several cabins and did some fishing before returning to the boat launch.

I think we spent several days fishing the upper Kenai, and they had plenty of fish to take home with them. I tried to smoke some of their salmon for them, but we weren't successful. Later we got really good at smoking salmon, and I send Roland some about every year. That's one thing he really likes.

GP, Frank and Roland with the day's catch

By the late 1970s the Kenai River was getting crowded. It was getting hard to fish with so many boats on the river. I think there were 300 or more guide boats on the river, not to mention the private boats.

I decided to fish in the salt water more so we could get away from the crowds. We would go to Seward and fish the Silver Salmon Derby in August. Don and I started going to the Chiswell Islands to fish but we soon found out that we were going to need a larger boat.

I sold my river boat in the late 70s and purchased a 21-foot cabin cruiser to use on the ocean. We were catching some really nice fish, and my brother-in-law Dennis Norris told me I should start a charter service. We considered this for a while, but the boat I had wasn't large enough to use as a charter boat. This is when we started looking for a suitable boat for a charter operation.

In 1981 I flew to Seattle to the glass ply boat manufacturing company to purchase a new custom-built boat. We settled on a 26-foot cabin cruiser with twin 140-horsepower, inboard engines. I was going to start a charter fishing service based at the Seward harbor. We decided on some basic rules for our charter operation that we still follow today. We wanted to provide the best and most comfortable trip possible for our customers. Our trips included sight seeing in the Kenai Fjords National Refuge, fishing, and generally having a good time. One of our rules was to throw back any halibut under 32 inches and any other fish that was under sized. We reasoned that if everyone followed these rules the fishing would continue to be good for many years to come.

We took delivery of the boat at Anchorage in September of 1982. It was too late to start the fishing season for that year. The boat turned out to be perfectly suited to what we were going to use it for. It had two large fish holds that were four feet long, two feet wide and twenty inches deep. The helm station was set up so that the captain was controlling the boat from a center-mounted seat with all of the controls within easy reach. There were two bench seats for the passengers on each side of the cabin. There was also a bunk and restroom located forward in the bow section. After deliberating for a few days we named the boat *Little Red* for my oldest daughter's hair color and size.

Little Red on her trailer

We decided to start our operations on Memorial Day and end the season on Labor Day. I went to the United States Coast Guard office in Anchorage and took the captain's test so I could run the boat legally with paying passengers onboard. My license was for carrying six passengers and one crew member while operating a vessel of no more than fifteen tons on the waters of Blying and Prince William Sound.

Little Red turned out to be an excellent rough-water vessel. She handled rough water better than any boat I had owned previously and brought us safely back to the harbor many times. There were days that we had to cancel charters because of storm conditions beyond what I felt safe in. Little Red's straight line length was 27 feet, and she was 10 feet wide. I think the center-mounted captains station helped because from here you could feel every movement the boat made.

By the time I decided to do this I had become familiar with nearly all of the waters in Alaska. I felt confident that I could be responsible for my own life and those of my passengers and crew. The waters here can really get bad, as I have stated before, and you have to pay attention to it at all times. There were trips where we had to find a protected bay and wait for the water to calm down before returning to port.

On one such trip we had been fishing in a protected cove, and when we started the trip back to the harbor the water turned bad on us, so I pulled into a protected cove to wait it out. One of the ladies on board told me she had to get home because her children were with a babysitter and would be worried. I told her that if we tried to get around the cape her kids would most likely become orphans.

We offered to call a charter float plane to take her in if it was really an emergency, which she declined. After that I called the harbor and had them contact her family. When the tide changed we were able to get around the cape and return to the harbor safely. This didn't happen very often, but sometimes the weather would fool you, and you'd get caught out in it. The best thing you can do in a situation like this is to find a sheltered cove and wait it out. A tide change can make a difference in all but the most extreme weather.

I remember another trip where we had 6 ministers on board. We were fishing for halibut and ling cod near the Chiswell Islands. They had been successful, and we exited the islands for the trip back to the harbor. When we cleared the islands there were six-foot swells with breakers on them in front of us. The angle of the swells were quartering the bow, and the boat was handling them without difficulty.

For some reason these ministers were spooked by the water conditions and began praying for God to deliver them from this tempest. I explained to them that we were in no danger; it was a little rough, but we would get back just fine. When we rounded the cape the roughness of the water picked up some, but the boat was handling it, and I still felt we weren't in any danger. That's when I heard one of the ministers tell God that if he would deliver him from this tempest he would never get on another boat again.

A private boat called me on the radio and asked me if he could follow us in. They were in a light aluminum boat about 20 feet in length with an eight-foot beam, eight feet wide. I told him to get in behind us and stay to the left of our wake where it would be a little better. I could tell by his voice on the radio that he was a little nervous.

We arrived at the harbor safely, and after filling our tank with gas we put Little Red into her slip. Once we were unloaded the preacher who made the promise to God told me they would see me next year. I had to tell him that they would have to go with someone else because of the promise he had made to God. I would have been afraid to take them out again. I believe that a promise to God is permanent, and it would be unwise to break it. He looked a little confused, but I think he knew what I meant.

The Coast Guard told me that a Williwaw occurs by cold air coming down from the high mountains. Apparently the lighter warm air rises from the low laying areas and holds back the heavier, cold air in the high mountains. When the conditions are just right the cold air will tear a hole in the warmer air, and it will roar down the mountain. The cold air will stay close to the ground or water until it has all been expelled.

On this trip I had a party from Hawaii fishing for silver salmon at Cains Head inside of Resurrection Bay. It was a beautiful sunny day, and the water was flat. There was no wind at all. There's an old World War II Army dock situated just behind Cains Head. Most of the dock had been destroyed during the 1964 earthquake but the pilings were still there sticking up out of the water.

We were having a good day and had caught a few silvers. I turned the boat to the south and had just started another pass across the point when the Coast Guard came on the radio's emergency channel and advised all boats to heave to, to the north. They said that a williwaw was going to come out of the north. Its winds would be in excess of

90 knots, and it was expected to last for 45 minutes. They repeated this message several times.

I told my passengers to bring in their lines and rack the rods in their holders. Then we all put on life jackets and I instructed them to remain seated until I told them otherwise. Then I turned Little Red's bow to the north as per the coast guards instructions. I could see the wind on the water coming up the bay in the distance. It was generating huge waves, and they were about to hit us head on. What made these waves so dangerous was that they were about 20 feet high and were only 20 feet apart. When they hit us the boat went up the first wave and dropped down into the trough. Little Red's bow went straight into the next wave before starting to climb up it. A huge amount of water hit the three large windows in front of me, and I thought they would break loose from their frames. Both of the bilge pumps came on to expel the water that was coming into the boat.

There must have been 600 gallons of water going over the boat. It would hit the windshields and go over the top of the boat and end up on the deck behind the cabin.

One of the ladies on board asked me if we were going to be okay, and I told her in as steady a voice as I could muster, "Yes, ma'am, I think so." By this time I had a plan of action formulated, and I told my customers about it. I told them if the windows failed I was going to turn the boat in a hard left turn and run it as far up on the beach as I could. Once there they would exit through the door to the bow, and jump off on the sandy beach. I believed that the pilings of the old dock would hold the boat long enough for them to get off. This would be a risky maneuver, but I felt like it could be done.

As it turned out I didn't have to beach the boat because the williwaw was weakening, and the water was calming down some.

When it was past and the Coast Guard gave the all clear I asked them if they wanted to continue fishing. The water was flat again. They told me they had had enough and wanted to get on solid ground again. I didn't tell them, but I felt the same. I have never been as scared as I was on that day.

113

Sometimes you'll have a trip that is so successful that it's hard to believe. This was one of those trips, and it would be hard to forget. One thing you should know about Pacific halibut is that the larger ones are dangerous. You can't bring one in the boat alive because it can break bones and tear up equipment when it's flopping around. We shoot all halibut above 40 pounds and make sure it's dead before we bring it aboard.

Our most memorable trip involved people visiting Alaska from Seattle, Washington. There were two elderly ladies and an elderly man who were visiting their nephews in Anchorage. They booked with us to fish for Pacific halibut and specified that we should take them to a place with calm water. That morning Tom and I decided to fish in Harris Bay about 60 miles south and west from the harbor. We had decided on Harris Bay because the water there is calm most of the time. Towards the back of Harris Bay there's a reef that runs nearly all the way across the bay. On the south side there is a passage over the reef that's about 50 yards wide and 20 feet deep. I positioned the boat in about 70 feet of water on the seaward side of this opening and told Tom to drop the anchor. When the anchor caught we noticed that the incoming tide was so fast that both of our propellers were turning as if we were still moving.

We were using 24-ounce cannon ball sinkers and large circle hooks that we had modified; the line was 100-pound Dacron. I took one of the rods and instructed our passengers on how to let the line out until they felt the sinker hit the bottom. I showed them how the reels functioned and set all of the drags so the line wouldn't break when a fish struck. The incoming tide had started to slow down some and that's when we got our first fish. It weighed around 100 pounds.

All of a sudden we had several fish on at the same time. It was hard to keep up with them. Both of the younger men had to stop fishing to assist their elderly family members because they couldn't bring these fish in by themselves. Between them they landed eight halibut and lost five or six others.

Our largest catch

Two other boats pulled up and anchored on each side of us about 50 feet away. Between both of them they only caught one fish. We must have anchored right over the halibut's migratory path, to the back of Harris Bay.

When we got back to the harbor and weighed the fish we had an impressive 1068 pounds of halibut with just eight fish. That meant that the average weight of each fish was 133.5 pounds. We hung the fish on a rack so the people could get some pictures. The weight of these fish collapsed the hanging rack just after we took this picture.

I don't know how hunting and fishing news found out about these fish, but they wanted a picture and an article for their paper. The local news papers also printed a story about this catch. I asked one of the ladies what they were going to do with all of this fish and she told me that Seattle was going to have one really big fish fry. At the time they caught these fish one of the ladies told me halibut was selling for $11.00 a pound in the grocery stores in Seattle. They had 855 pounds of filet. That's $9,400.00 dollars worth of halibut. I have provided picture's of this catch to many people who have asked for it. This was the largest catch ever brought in on our charter boat. We ran our charter service for 16 years in Seward and took thousands of people fishing from all over the world.

My son Tom ran Little Red for several years, and he was a good, competent captain.

I hired several captains to run the boat when I wasn't available to run it. They were all good men and followed the rules I had set up for *Little Red*. The best skipper I ever had was my son Tom. He crewed on the boat for years and learned a great deal about fishing from me. He used what he learned and added to it his own theories and became the best fisherman in Seward. (*I still think he's the best.*) When Tom went in to the coast guard to get his license he ended up with a better license than I had. His license stated that he could operate a 150-ton vessel while carrying 20 passengers on the waters of Blying and Prince William Sound. This is an impressive license.

Tom had decided to fish off of Montague Island close to San Juan Bay. On this trip he limited six passengers with nearly every game fish in Prince William Sound. The holds were full and fish were all over the deck when they came into the harbor. He had six passengers on board at the time, and they were all amazed at the number of fish they had caught. It must have been a lot of fun for them and some work, too. They were probably very tired after this trip.

Halibut is the fish that most people want when they book a charter, but sometimes halibut won't cooperate. When this occurred we would fish for ling cod and black rockfish. The ling cod in my opinion is as good to eat as the halibut, and they are much easier to catch. Ling cod can weigh as much as 70 pounds, and we have seen some that would weigh more than that. We called black rock fish "bass," and they ranged in size from four pounds up to eight pounds. I have seen some that weighed 15 pounds. Later in the season silver salmon show up in good numbers and are really fun to catch.

On this trip Tom had limited his customers with all four of these species' of fish. Each person on the boat excluding the skipper and crew was limited to two halibut, two ling cod, 10 bass, and six silver salmon. (*The skipper and crew members are not allowed to fish with customers on board.*) They came in with 12 large halibut, 12 large ling cod, 60 better than average bass, and 36 good silver salmon. I've never heard of anyone doing this before this trip. They had 120 fish on the boat when they finished the day's fishing. I can't even imagine how busy they must have been that day. During this particular season Tom managed to repeat the same thing many times with different groups of people on board. They were all amazed and thought Tom was the best skipper they had ever seen.

On this trip I was privileged to see the largest halibut I have ever seen. I've seen 400 pound halibut, but this one was a lot bigger than that.

I had six young men on this trip. They were in their late 20s or early 30s. I decided to take them to a mound located towards the back of Aialik Bay. Located about 35 miles south and west of the harbor, they told me that they wanted to catch some large halibut. This mound had produced some good fish, and I felt like it would be a good place to start.

When we arrived at the mound I set up their rods and started fishing in the 30 feet of water on top of the mound. I had baited their hooks with whole salmon heads, which is what we used for the larger halibut. The tide was ebbing on an incoming tide and was starting out, so our drift was towards the outlet of Aialik Bay.

We were drifting down a fairly steep slope to the 300-foot mark before reeling in and starting another drift. On one of these drifts one of the poles bent almost double, and I asked him if he was hung up on the bottom. He told me, no, he thought it was a fish so I let the boat drift a little farther and watched his pole. When the pole had bent over I looked at the depth finder and noted that we were in 200 feet of water.

Something didn't look right with this situation, I asked him again if he was feeling anything on his line. He told me that every once in a while he felt it pull and the drag on his reel slipped, letting line out. He still had plenty of line on the reel, so I looked at the depth finder again and saw we were now in 600 feet of water. I told him that I was going to try and keep the boat positioned over the fish so that his line would be straight down. I knew that if he kept pulling at an angle he would loose this fish.

He fought this fish until his arms were so tired that he wanted one of his friends to take over for a while. I told these guys that they probably weren't going to get this fish and asked them if they wanted to cut the line and get one that would be more manageable. They talked it over and decided that they wanted to keep at it until they got it, or it broke off. These guys were changing back and forth on the rod for over six hours before they started gaining on this fish. I had no idea what kind of fish they had hooked, but I knew that it was very large.

I took this time to tell these guys a little of what I had learned about the Pacific halibut. One of our Local Fish and Game biologists told me that halibut don't gain much weight when they're small. He said that most of the smaller halibut are male and most of the larger ones are female. He told me that he has heard of commercially caught halibut weighing in at 700 pounds, and that they could live to be 55 years old. The largest one caught by a sport fisherman was 459 pounds; it was caught in 1996.

Halibut fight different from most fish; they usually want to stay on the bottom. They will give a series of strong pulls that will take out line on their way back down to the bottom. The smaller ones will stroke their tails fast, and the line that leaves the reel will come off in a quick series of three- or four-foot lengths. The larger they are the more line they pull off when they stroke their tails. This one was pulling off 10 feet of line every time she moved her tail, and it didn't come off fast; it came off slow and steady with each stroke of her tail.

They were finally getting the fish up close to the surface. She had to be tired from pulling on that line for as long as she did. When we saw her it was apparent that we would never be able to get her into the boat, she was just too big. I don't have any idea how big she was, but she was at least five feet wide, maybe more. She was so long that she wouldn't fit into the boat, and if these guys wanted to keep her she would have to be towed back to the harbor. I told them that it would be a shame to kill this fish just for bragging rights. It was their decision to make, and I would have killed her and towed her to the harbor if that was what they wanted.

To my surprise they elected to take some pictures and let her go. I didn't get any pictures and have regretted it to this day. After they took their pictures one of them reached over and cut the line. As she drifted slowly down I marveled at how beautiful she was. It was late in the day, and these fellows were worn out, so we returned to the harbor. When we were tied up to the slip I returned the money they had paid me for the charter. I have never seen another group of people who were better sportsmen than these fellows were. If I had to estimate the size of this fish I would have to say it was at least 500 pounds plus, and that's a low estimate. Over the years we've hooked many very large halibut but this was the only one we were able to bring to the surface.

In the Kenai Fjords there are many different kinds of wildlife and birds, and on most trips you will see some of them. There will be killer whales, large humpback whales, sea lions, seals, salmon sharks, porpoises, and many different types of birds, including the Arctic puffin. I highly recommend a trip to the Kenai fiords if you visit Alaska. There are several large cruise boats that visit this area every day during the summer. If you want to go fishing, the charter booking services in Seward can recommend a good boat for you.

I am no longer chartering in Seward. We shut down our charter operation in the late 90s and sold *Little Red*. In all the years that we ran our charter service no one was ever injured, and we were never towed back to the harbor. None of our customers were ever dissatisfied with our service, and we never came in without fish. It is an impressive record that we are extremely are proud of. It would be impossible to relate to you all of the different trips we made. I can only tell you that every one of them was different, and every one of them contained its own story. Anyone who ever went on our charter will always remember the trip. This was one of the most satisfying periods of my life in Alaska, and I will never forget it.

Recreational gold mining is a lot of fun, and we just had to try it.

Don and I got the gold fever and decided to try mining, so we purchased a small suction dredge and two good metal detectors. Both of us were looking forward to finding the mother lode. Of course that didn't happen, but we had a lot of fun trying anyway. Don and I have used the metal detectors all over the Kenai Peninsula but we never found anything. I suppose we need more experience in using them. We've used the dredge at Eureka, Petersville, and at several streams on the peninsula with the same results. We did find some very fine gold flakes, but they didn't amount to much.

One year my son in-law, his son Steven, and I went to a place called Bachelor Creek north of Fairbanks. To get there we drove from Soldotna to Fairbanks on the new Parks Highway, a distance of 507 miles. Once we arrived in Fairbanks we drove an additional 80 miles north on the Steese Highway to the state maintenance yard. At the state maintenance yard we turned left and found the trail going up the mountains towards Bachelor Creek.

This is a good trail, but I would not advise trying to travel on it in anything but a four-wheel-drive vehicle. The trail was dry until we descended into the valley, where it was muddy and soft. After crossing a small, unnamed creek we came out on Bachelor Creek. There is a mining road that runs along the side of Bachelor Creek and crosses it in several places.

In earlier times this creek had been mined with a commercial dredge, and the bed rock was left exposed. There are large piles of tailings in several places, and one of them has divided the creek so that it runs around it. We put up our camp next to one of the tailing piles not too far from the creek. I think we spent 10 days here, and the weather was beautiful. It got up into the 90s every day.

The next morning we decided to look around before doing any mining, and there was quite a bit to see. There was an old cabin on the left side of the creek with an outhouse behind it. At several places we saw pieces of iron that had been cut off of the dredge and left where they fell. The dredge has left a huge scar on the landscape, but it is recovering. Large dredges like the one used here usually miss a lot of gold, and people find quite a bit of it here.

There's a story told of one woman who came here with a gold pan and a shovel in 1955. They say she stayed here all summer before going back to Fairbanks. The story says that when she got to Fairbanks she sold her gold and had enough money to buy herself a new Cadillac. She mined on the tailing pile that divides the creek, and today people call it Cadillac pile. I don't know if this story is true or not, but I have heard it from several different people.

We dredged at several likely places along the creek, and every time we cleaned up we had some gold. What we got was mostly fines, but there were enough of them to keep us interested, and we kept at it. The problem we were having was that the suction of our dredge was only one-and-one-half inches; it was too small. When we go back up there we plan on having a five-inch dredge, and we feel confident we'll find some nuggets. One man we talked to showed us seven nice nuggets and a couple of small bottles with a good amount of fine gold in them. He had been there for seven days and was using a four-inch dredge.

If you come to Alaska and want to pan or dredge for gold, the state requires that you get a permit. They don't cost anything, but if you are checked you must have one on you. There are several places where you can pay to pan for gold without a permit. I recommend old dredge number eight located just outside of Fairbanks. It's an old dredge that the state has turned into a museum. There is a small fee to get in. Once you are inside and have taken the tour they will give you material from the tailings that will contain gold. Another place is the tour at the Eldorado Mine. They guarantee gold in every bag they sell to you.

I want to give you a word of caution here; if you are going to be out anywhere north of Fairbanks bring along a hat, gloves, a long-sleeved shirt, and a good mosquito net. The mosquitoes will come at you in huge clouds when the sun isn't out. They won't bother you much when the sun is shining on you. These are must-have items.

Riding Snow Machines in Alaska is our favorite winter activity, and we have ridden across much of Alaska.

I started riding snow machines in earnest just a few years after we settled in Alaska. It's one of those things that you have to learn. My first few attempts were more than likely very funny to watch. The snow machines that were around in 1966 weren't anything like the ones on the market today. Don was the one who introduced me to them, and the first machine I owned I bought from him. It was a black scorpion with red stripes on it. I don't think they even make them today. The motor was small, and the track was narrow and short. It was very tippy.

During those first years Don and I liked to go out on Tustumena Lake when it had frozen hard and was safe to ride on. These were memorable trips. Most of the time we spent the night in one of the old cabins on the lake shore. This lake would sometimes have open leads on it so we had to be extremely careful where we rode. The ice on the lake is the same color as the water is during the summer. Sometimes we would come up on places where ice heaves had occurred. These ice heaves were setting on the lake and were about 10 feet high. This is some of the most beautiful ice I have ever seen. Its color was a turquoise blue.

The local snow machine clubs used to put on annual races from Soldotna to Homer and back. It was usually a two-day event and was called the Kenai 200: the distance being 200 miles to Homer and back. These races were run from the late 1960s through the late 1970s. I think they were stopped because of the possibility of lawsuits if property was damaged or someone was injured. Don and I ran several of these races. We never won anything, but they were fun anyway. Most of the race was run off of the roads along power lines or on seismograph trails. Sometimes it was necessary to bring it out to the highway to refuel the machines. There was a lot of participation from the communities, and hundreds of people lined the roads to watch their favorite racers go by. I don't know of anyone ever being injured, but there was some damage to private property along the route. On most of the races the temperature was below zero, and with temperatures this low it was a little uncomfortable.

By far the most enjoyable riding was when we went with family members on extended trips around Alaska. Caribou hills are located between Soldotna and Homer near the mountains, and this is an excellent place to ride. There are several trails leading to Caribou Hill from east of Homer and at Clam Gulch. Many people over the years have built cabins in Caribou Hills so they can spend more time there. This is also a favorite hunting area for the local residents and others from around the state.

As time went on we decided to go only when the temperature was above freezing. This was a good decision, and the riding became more enjoyable. We liked to go up to Eureka Lodge and rent a room for several days. The snow machining behind the lodge offers trails that go for miles, and the hill climbing is excellent here.

Like any other outdoor sport you must exercise caution whenever you ride in mountainous terrain. Alaska has lost many people to avalanches; the snow is deep, and when the temperature and other conditions are just right they will occur. If you're going to participate in this sport it's a must to watch the weather and check with the authorities on the snow conditions. You should also a let someone else know where you are going to be. Dress warmly and try to keep dry to avoid hypothermia. Hypothermia kills a lot of people every year, and it is a condition that can be avoided. One of my rules has been to never ride alone. *That's inviting trouble*. I broke my own rule that day on Sports Lake and I have never broken it since.

Post Script

Alaska has changed considerably since I came here in 1965. All of the communities mentioned in this book have doubled and then tripled and tripled again. The trip from Seattle to Anchorage only takes three hours now, and the airport in Anchorage has grown to an unbelievable size. It has everything any airport in the lower 48 states has and seems to be under construction all the time. The Kenai airport is now a modern facility and has good runways and many services to offer the public. Soldotna and Homer have also upgraded their airports.

On the Kenai Peninsula all the highways have been upgraded and paved. Nearly all of the streets in the cities have been paved. You will find all of the same things in our cities that you would find in any city in the lower 48 states. Stop signs and lights are numerous, and convenience stores are everywhere. All of the Kenai River boat launching facilities and campgrounds have improved and are hardly recognizable from what they used to be.

The Kenai River is recognized around the world for its king salmon fishing. All of the guide services on the river have improved, and I have been told their catch ratio of king salmon is very good. Even Cooper Landing has grown, and they offer fishing trips and white-water rafting.

There are still plenty of areas that are not as densely populated, and you can still get away from the crowds if you want to. When I started my charter service in Seward there were from five to eight charters operating there. Today there are probably around 70 charter services there. It's the same in the Homer harbor, but I think there are more charter boats here than in Seward.

I'm still pretty active for my age and plan on having many more adventure in Alaska.

My son, son in-law and I have purchased a new boat and still fish, mostly in the ocean. Dennis still has his river boat and occasionally we will fish on the upper Kenai River. Our next big trip will be on the Yukon and Koyukuk Rivers to hunt for moose and explore the interior of Alaska. We will use our boat on this trip and will travel several hundred miles on the rivers. I am looking forward to it.

May God bless you and may you follow your dreams no matter where they take you.